BROKEN
TRUST

**Center Point
Large Print**

**This Large Print Book carries the
Seal of Approval of N.A.V.H.**

BROKEN TRUST

Sharon Dunn

CENTER POINT LARGE PRINT
THORNDIKE, MAINE

This Center Point Large Print edition is published
in the year 2012 by arrangement with
Harlequin Books S.A.

The text of this Large Print edition is unabridged.
In other aspects, this book may
vary from the original edition.
Printed in the United States of America
on permanent paper.
Set in 16-point Times New Roman type.

ISBN: 978-1-61173-386-0

Library of Congress Cataloging-in-Publication Data

Dunn, Sharon, 1965–
Broken trust / Sharon Dunn. — Large print ed.
p. cm. — (Center Point large print edition)
ISBN 978-1-61173-386-0 (library binding : alk. paper)
1. Large type books. I. Title.
PS3604.U57B76 2012
813′.6—dc23

2012003140

Commit your way to the Lord;
trust in him and he will do this:
He will make your righteousness
shine like the dawn,
the justice of your cause
like the noonday sun.
—*Psalms* 37:5–6

For my children who
inspire and challenge me
to be a better person

BROKEN TRUST

ONE

Commit your way to the Lord; trust in Him and He will do this: He will make your righteousness shine like the dawn, the justice of your cause like the noonday sun.

Psalm 37: 5–6

Special Agent Wyatt Green knew he was in trouble even before he felt the bone in his arm crack. Unexpected high winds had caused the helicopter he was supposed to drop out of to pitch to one side.

When he was almost down the rope, he'd lost his grip, twisted in the air and held his hands out to brace his fall. The impact with the ground sent shivers of pain up both his arms, but there was no mistaking that splintering of bone. He suspected a fractured forearm. As he rose to his feet, he told himself it wasn't that bad. He'd broken bones clean through, and the pain from that was even more mind-numbing. He'd completed assignments with injuries before, and he could do it again.

As the helicopter disappeared into the night sky and the thrum of the motor became more distant, Wyatt gritted his teeth against the pain and got his bearings. The badlands of eastern Montana looked just as remote and foreboding at night as they did in the daytime. Ten years ago, he and a team of agents had descended on this same area for a standoff with a landowner who appeared to be amassing an army to help him carry out his domestic terrorist philosophy.

A pain more intense than the fracture jabbed at his heart. Ten years ago, Agent Christine Norris, barely out of the academy, had walked away from a career to marry a rancher in this area. She'd also walked away from him. A flash of memory, Christine's easy laugh and soft brown eyes, caused him to lose focus. He shook off the emotional ache, adjusted his backpack, checked his coordinates and headed toward where Christine and Dustin's farmhouse was supposed to be.

Ignoring the pain in his arm, he jogged at a steady pace along the dirt road. When his supervisor picked him for this mission, he hadn't argued. Ten-year-old wounds that still felt raw were hardly grounds for refusing an assignment. He was a professional. He had experience in this part of the country. He could manage his feelings about Christine just fine. It had taken him years to accept it, but their relationship had fallen apart because of him. She was a married woman now. He had to let it go and focus on work.

He stopped for a moment to look at the

photograph of five-year-old Tyler Lansky. When he clicked on his flashlight, Tyler's gap-toothed grin and blond hair came into view. Tyler was the reason he had been sent back here. Emmett Lansky had taken Tyler during a custody battle. Emmett had ties to a militia group believed to be setting up a training camp in this area.

The Bureau had been watching Emmett for quite some time. Now that Emmett had broken his custody agreement and taken his son across state lines, they had the excuse they needed to move in and make an arrest. Any intel out of him would be a step in the right direction. Though getting Tyler home safe to his mom was their primary mission, the infiltration would allow the FBI to see if there was any truth to the chatter they had been hearing, that this particular group was planning activities that fell outside the law.

Headlights flashed across Wyatt's field of vision. He dived off the road into some brush. Lying low in the tall grass, he waited while the old pickup chugged past. Unusual to see someone out on a country road this late at night. His supervisor had warned Wyatt to keep the mission as quiet as possible. They didn't want a repeat of what had happened ten years ago when they had shown up in full force, for what probably could have been a one- or two-agent operation. The rancher had turned out to be way more talk than action. The real tragedy was that after a forty-two-

11

day siege, an agent had shot a fourteen-year-old boy who was climbing the fence of the property. The group had run out of water, and the boy was taking a bucket down to the river. The FBI sniper, exhausted from lack of sleep and restless from days of inactivity, had mistaken the bucket for a weapon.

The encounter had left the locals with a bitter taste in their mouths and a distrust of the FBI. This time they were only sending Wyatt and his partner. If a team or experts were needed, they could pull them from field and satellite offices fast enough.

Wyatt waited until the taillights of the old truck disappeared over a hill before resuming his jog down the road. He ran with an easy stride, barely out of breath. Early spring in Montana meant there was still a chill in the night air.

Dropping in by night would allow his partner in the helicopter to do a search for lights in remote places that might indicate a camp. The pilot would swing back around and get him. If the helicopter located anything or Christine gave them a direction to go, they would have an easy in and an easy out. No contact with townspeople required, no reopening of old wounds.

Christine had been a part of this community for ten years, and she'd recently been elected sheriff. She had to know something.

Wyatt slowed the pace of his jogging as

memories rushed at him. She had been truly happy when she met Dustin. She probably had half a dozen kids by now. After a while, he'd been happy for her. She deserved it. His only regret was that he hadn't been the man to make her happy. Working for the Bureau was what had kept them together, and he hadn't seen what a gem Christine was until he'd lost her.

He ran to the top of the hill. In the distance, the lights from a farmhouse and outbuildings came into view. After tossing his backpack over a barbed-wire fence, he climbed it and made his way through a field filled with cattle. Most of the heifers had bedded down for the night with their calves. Those who were standing weren't fazed as he passed by them.

As he neared the farmhouse, he felt a tightening in his chest that made it hard to breathe.

"Mommy, I saw lights." Five-year-old Eva stood in the doorway of the old kitchen.

Christine looked up from the stack of bills she'd been shuffling through. Jake, their border collie, stirred at her feet. "Honey, you're supposed to be in bed." Every time she looked at Eva, she saw Dustin in her light brown curly hair and round eyes.

"But I saw lights in the sky, Mama." She clutched the worn stuffed animal a little tighter. "Do you think it was angels coming to tell us about Daddy?" The little girl's expression was hopeful and bright.

The only one having a harder time with losing Dustin than Christine was Eva. Her daughter hadn't slept through the night since her father died in a hay-baler accident over a year ago. Christine's heart squeezed tight, but she managed a smile. "I don't know if angels need lights to see by. Come get one more hug, sweetie, and then it's off to bed for you."

Eva slipped easily into her mother's arms. Christine held her, burying her face in the soft hair and inhaling the sweet little-girl smell.

"Everything all right?" Grandma Maggie, Dustin's mother, stood in the doorway. Her gray hair was braided into a single rope that fell over her shoulder. Time spent in her garden had made Maggie's skin a rich brown.

"We're doing just fine." Christine squeezed Eva a little tighter, enjoying the warmth of the hug. "Eva thought she saw some lights in the sky."

"I saw them, too," said Maggie.

Christine sat up a little straighter. "Really." She'd been willing to dismiss the lights as Eva's imagination; everything and anything, real and imagined, seemed to wake that poor child up, but if Maggie had seen the lights, too . . .

"When I got up to get a glass of water during the commercial for my program, I saw them through the bathroom window to the north," said Maggie.

Christine stood up and set Eva on the worn linoleum. "Why don't you have Grandma Maggie put you to bed?"

Maggie held out her arms. "How about Grandma tells you a story to help you sleep?"

Eva clapped her hands together and ran to her grandma. Christine listened while their voices faded down the hallway before returning to her bills. Through the open window in the kitchen, the cows in the corral mooed and bustled. Jake lifted his head and then rose to his feet, emitting one quick, sharp bark as he faced the north door.

Something was stirring things up out there. "I suppose we ought to go check it out, huh?"

The dog's light blue eyes seemed to hold some understanding of what she was saying. He twisted his head to one side as though agreeing with her. With Jake trailing behind her, Christine made her way into the living room where Grandma Maggie had been watching a home-improvement show. As she grabbed the shotgun off the fireplace mantel, she could hear the soft murmur of the older woman's voice and Eva's laughter down the hallway.

Three females living alone with the nearest neighbor five miles down the road had the potential to make Christine feel vulnerable, but she could take care of herself. Her training at the FBI academy, endless firearms instruction and years spent hunting with Dustin had given her that confidence.

She pushed the door open, closing it softly behind her and stepping into the night. Heavy cloud cover meant no moonlight or stars. She stepped away from the circle of illumination the porch light created. As she neared the barn, the aroma of hay and livestock greeted her. Dustin had loved it out here, and she had grown to love it. Dustin's old horse still seemed restless as it clopped around the corral. The pigs in the barn were snorting louder than usual for this hour. A raccoon or a coyote might have gotten in there. The last thing she needed was to have half her chickens be some varmint's dinner. The ranch barely broke even. She couldn't afford the loss.

Jake brushed against Christine's leg. The dog stopped suddenly. The hair on his back bristled, and he emitted a low growl.

"Easy, boy." Her heartbeat revved up a notch. Her nerves tingled in anticipation of an encounter. Inside the chicken house, it didn't sound like an all-out massacre was taking place. The fox or coyote or whatever it was must be close, though, because the clucking and flapping of wings indicated some alarm had gone off for the birds.

She soothed the dog as they drew closer to the barn. Jake's yipping became repetitive and higher pitched the closer they got to the side of the barn. She held the rifle at her side but was prepared to lift it and look through the sight at a second's notice. Holding her breath, she placed one foot in front of the other.

She startled when a shadow stepped out from behind the barn, a man. His hands went up in a surrender gesture.

She gripped the rifle a little tighter, but didn't aim it. Most likely it was a farmer who had broken down on the road. "What are you doing here? Can I help you?"

The man uttered a single word. "Christine."

Christine nearly fell backward as memories hit her like a tidal wave. She knew that voice. "Wyatt?"

He stepped closer to her, which caused Jake to rapid-fire bark and bounce from side to side.

"Jake, give it a rest." Christine narrowed her eyes at the dog. The dog came to a sitting position beside her. His tail still twitched—an indication that he was ready to mount another assault of barking and bouncing.

Christine stared at the man in front of her, barely visible in the minimal light. What do you say to a man you thought you loved once upon a time? They had worked together and dated for almost two years. He was the one who had convinced her to apply to the FBI. And she had waited and hoped for a marriage proposal, waited and hoped for him to say he loved her, too. By the time she got her first field assignment ten miles from here in Roosevelt, she'd broken up with him knowing that he would never take the next step in their relationship . . . and then God had brought Dustin into her life. "What are you doing here?"

"It's work related. I need your help," he said.

"Work related?" Without knowing why, she found herself digging her heels in, feeling reluctant to invite him into her house. She'd have to explain who he was to Grandma Maggie and Eva if they were still up. "Why didn't you just contact me at my office? You do know I'm the sheriff for Mohler County?"

"We're trying to do this mission with as little disruption to the community as possible because of what happened ten years ago." He took a step toward her. "It's awful dark out here, don't you think? Can we go inside and talk?"

When she'd met Dustin, she had left Wyatt and her past behind. She'd grown up in a Christian home, but Wyatt's charm had caught her up in a whirlwind. Maybe she just didn't want to revisit that part of her life again—maybe that was what the reluctance was about.

Wyatt rubbed his forearm and winced.

Even in the dim light, she could see that he was in pain. A rush of sympathy caused her to step toward him. "Did you hurt yourself?"

He shrugged. "Just landed funny, is all."

The way he tried to hide the pain tugged at her

heart. He always had to be a tough guy. "I suppose you can come inside and at least get a cold compress on that." She led him to the back door and into the kitchen. The television was still on in the next room, but she didn't know if Maggie had gone back to her program or not.

Still not feeling at ease, she turned toward the stove and twisted one of the knobs. The gas flame shot out, and she placed the kettle on it. "Have a chair. Can I get you a cup of hot tea or something?" After a quick intake of breath, she angled her head to look at him.

Wyatt waved the suggestion away with a hand. "I won't take up too much of your time. I am sure you have family to attend to." Instead of taking a chair, Wyatt wandered around the kitchen. He had never been one to sit still.

He hadn't changed much in ten years, same muscular build, same hardened features. No gray showed yet in the jet-black hair. The other agents had nicknamed him "Street Fighter." Two years in the military had made Wyatt Green disciplined and clean-cut, but something about him would always echo the tough streets of Las Vegas where he'd grown up.

Christine searched her freezer for the cold compresses with no luck. "I think my daughter has been taking the compresses for her stuffed animals. Frozen corn will do in a pinch." She tossed it to him.

He caught the bag of corn and pressed it against his forearm. "Whatever works."

She studied him for a moment, the angles and planes of his face, his square jaw. Only the tightening of his mouth gave away that he was hurting. "I know a little first aid. Let me have a look at it."

"Be my guest." He set the bag of frozen vegetables aside and held his arm out to her. Cupping his elbow, she palpated up his forearm. His skin was warm to the touch. She stood close enough to be engulfed in the soapy, clean scent. Her heartbeat quickened a little. She had always liked that smell.

"Ouch." He winced and drew back, massaging the spot where she had pressed hard. "Thanks a lot, Nurse Christine."

She smiled. "Don't be such a baby. You definitely did something to it, but I don't think it is broken. You probably just bruised or twisted it." She handed him the bag of corn. "See if this helps at all."

Silence descended between them. Christine freshened her cup of tea from the kettle that simmered on the stove. "So why has the Bureau sent you back here in such a clandestine way?"

Wyatt paced around the kitchen table as though he were trying to formulate how to answer her question. He stopped to examine a picture of Dustin and Christine standing in front of a row of

20

tall sunflowers. She thought to tell him about the accident, but changed her mind. She felt the need to be guarded around him. The less personal they had to get, the better.

Wyatt didn't say anything, but he flexed his hand and his jawline hardened. When he turned around to face her, he smiled. She knew him too well. The smile was an attempt to hide the pain that seeing the picture had caused. Even though they'd had to work the Roosevelt assignment together, she'd broken up with Wyatt before she had met Dustin. All Wyatt's hurt over the breakup had come out as anger, which only confirmed that he was not emotionally mature enough to make any kind of a commitment to her. It didn't look as if he'd changed much in the past ten years. He still buried his feelings.

She repeated her request. "You said you were here on agency business."

Wyatt cleared his throat and squared his shoulders. "Yes, we have reason to believe that a man has taken his son to a militia training camp somewhere in this area. Emmett Lansky violated the conditions of his custody agreement when he took the boy across state lines. He was only supposed to have the kid for the weekend."

Her breath caught in her throat. Handling the cases that involved children was always hard for her. "How old is the little boy?"

"He's five."

The same age as Eva. Christine set her cup of tea on the table as shock waves vibrated through her. She only hoped they made getting the child back their top priority. "Let me guess, though. The violation of the custody agreement allows you to gather some intel on this group and gives you some leverage for making Lansky talk. So far, you haven't been able to catch them doing anything illegal, but you suspect they are up to something."

"That kid needs to be back with his mom," Wyatt said. "That's the focus of the assignment."

Christine pressed a little. "But you have probably been watching this guy, waiting for him to break some law, so you will at the very least have a reason to question him."

"We've had eyes on Lansky and the group he's a leader of for a long time. They are anti-government, and judging from some emails we intercepted, they may be planning on doing harm to some elected officials they don't like. It could just be talk, but we'd like to prevent an escalation. The normal pattern is for them to start looking for ways to fund their plans, usually through some illegal activity. If we can prevent that, we will have done our job." He made his way around the kitchen table. "Either way, the kid gets home safe to his mom, and we rein in Emmett, which might cause the other members to back off."

She crossed her arms and shook her head. "I just hope that little boy is okay."

His expression became serious. "I intend to do everything I can to get that kid back in his mother's arms." He tapped his fingers on the table. "It's not a bad thing if we're able to prevent an act of domestic terrorism in the process."

"I'm glad you take your job so seriously." Wyatt's strong need for justice had been one of the things that had drawn her to him in the first place. It was an admirable quality, but not enough to base a life together on. "I can't say that I miss it—the agency, I mean."

He stepped toward her. His eyes were full of fire. "Too bad. You had a nice start on being a great agent." His voice had grown husky.

She could read the smoldering undercurrent of attraction in his words. He wasn't really talking about her skills as an agent. He was talking about them, about their relationship. As always, though, Wyatt could never directly say how he felt, and she had to try to decipher the code he spoke in. Some things never changed. "I still have a lot to do tonight. What do you need from me?"

"You know the area. You know the people, and you are the sheriff. These guys must have built some ties to people around here. They may even have recruited members from the town. I need you to tell me of any people who have said things that sounded like they had a beef with the government. Anyone who has had long, unexplained absences that might indicate they're

23

at the camp. Has anyone been purchasing a lot of firearms? You know what to look for. If we could bring in a person who would give up the location of the camp, the assignment would be completed in two or three days."

Christine felt herself growing defensive. He was asking her to betray the people she loved and cared about without cause or true evidence. She wasn't about to point the finger at anyone just because of an offhand remark. "With airplanes, helicopters and cutting-edge surveillance equipment at your disposal, you can't find one little training camp. Maybe it doesn't exist."

"You know better than I do that there are a thousand places a group of men could hide out here," he asserted.

Christine pressed the palms of her hands together in an attempt to hide the rising anger. "You don't understand these people. There's a big difference between men who support each other and practice target shooting and men who are plotting to overthrow the government. Just because someone owns a gun and complains about paying taxes doesn't make them an outlaw."

An edginess entered Wyatt's voice. "Look, we messed up bad ten years ago, I know that. We thought we would be a little more low-key this time. That's why I came to you. I need your help."

"The mistake the agency made ten years ago wasn't just that poor kid getting shot. We came in as outsiders. We treated these good people like they were either stupid country folk or extremists. I'm not an outsider anymore. I can tell you these are good people here, smart and hard-working. They don't want extremists here any more than you do."

"I'm trying to protect the good people, too," Wyatt insisted.

She stepped toward him. "These are my people now. They've put their trust in me when they elected me sheriff. I'm not going to betray them because one of them might have complained about the government at a church potluck."

"I'm not saying they are bad people. I'm just saying sometimes there can be some rotten apples. And the bad guys look and act just like the good guys."

"And what if I point the finger at somebody, and it turns out I'm wrong?" Christine set her teacup on the table. "I'll do everything I can to help you get that child back, but I won't make accusations without solid evidence. Reputation is everything around here. People are going to know if someone is brought in for questioning, and it won't matter if the guy turned out to be innocent."

"Mommy, I heard voices." Eva stood in the doorway holding her favorite stuffed bear.

Christine swooped Eva up in her arms. "Sweetie, you are supposed to be in bed."

Eva pointed to Wyatt. "Who are you?"

"He's just an . . . old friend who came to ask Mommy for help she can't give." She couldn't prevent the steely look she gave him.

"What kind of help?"

Christine rubbed noses with Eva. "You ask too many questions." Her attempt at being playful sounded hollow. Wyatt had her so stirred up she probably wasn't going to sleep at all tonight. "I have to put my daughter back to bed."

"Good, I'll just see myself out." His voice lacked the defensiveness she had expected. Instead, she picked up on something conciliatory in his tone.

"Come on, Eva." She took her daughter's hand and led her down the hallway. As Christine settled Eva beneath her yellow quilt, she heard the door open and close. She kissed Eva and touched her sweet nose with her finger. "Now, for the last time, my dear, go to bed."

She closed the door to Eva's room and returned to the kitchen. Wyatt had left the bag of frozen corn on the table. She rushed outside. He stood at the end of the stone walkway, holding a phone in his hand.

"You can take this if it helps the pain in your arm." His soft response had caused her to regret her own irritation.

"Thanks, and it'll give me something to eat later."

She smiled at his joke. "I didn't mean to be so

26

reactionary to your request. It's just that . . . this is where I belong now."

"Don't worry about it. I understand." The inflection in his voice seemed to communicate the exact opposite of what he said. He was hurt on a personal level by her reluctance to help.

"You helicoptered in, right? That was the lights we saw."

He nodded. "We thought that would be quicker and less noticeable than a truck that nobody recognized."

"So they are coming back for you?"

He waggled the phone. "Already got a rendezvous point established. Just got to hike out there." Again, the tone of his voice betrayed him. She could detect the hurt underneath.

How easy it was to fall back into an old pattern. Why did she even care about his feelings? She let out a sigh, crossed her arms against the spring cold and said, "I hope you are able to find the little boy . . . but I really don't think he's around here. There are other sheriffs in other counties. They may have seen something." Again, she resented the position he had put her in. Still, the thought of the little boy separated from his mom pierced through her. "Of course, as the sheriff, I am obligated to cooperate . . . and I will if it is needed."

Wyatt didn't say anything, only pivoted and started jogging. As she listened to his footsteps fade in the distance, her emotions stirred up all over again. Only this time, she was upset with herself for the renewed intensity of attraction for a man she thought she would never see again.

TWO

Wyatt closed his Bible and massaged his chest where an intense ache had plagued him ever since he had left Christine's. He had wanted to justify himself to her. To let her know that he was not the man she had dated ten years ago. But seeing the picture of Dustin with his arms wrapped around her had given him pause. She was a married woman. He questioned his motives in wanting her to view him in a different light . . . and knew he needed to back off.

His partner, Samuel Cranson, opened the motel-room door and stuck his head in. "Nice morning out there. Ready to go?" Samuel was almost twenty years Wyatt's senior and close to retirement.

Wyatt tossed the Bible on top of his suitcase and rose to his feet after grabbing a wrap for his injured forearm. He didn't have time to find a doctor. If he'd cracked a bone, it would mend on its own. "Let's hope we get some kind of lead."

The two men got into a battered pickup that

had been purchased for them at a sheriff's sale one county over. He doubted the pickup would fool anyone. In a town as small as Roosevelt, every stranger stood out like a sore thumb.

The plan had been made for Wyatt to try to probe Christine's brain one more time while Samuel started questioning the law enforcement in neighboring counties. So much for easy in, easy out. Their investigation had just gone a little more aboveboard. Hopefully, though, no one would peg them as federal agents.

The safety of the little boy was not an issue. All the reports and even the ex-wife confirmed that Emmett doted on his son. Since it had been a point of contention in the divorce proceedings, Emmett's desire to raise the little boy with the radical views had probably prompted him to take his son. The urgency came in finding the camp before the members found out they had been located and Emmett had a chance to find a new hiding place.

As they drove the few miles from the roadside motel into town, his thoughts returned to Christine. Ten years ago, he'd taken her for granted. He'd messed up. The better man had gotten her. Seeing her last night with her daughter was a cruel reminder of what he had missed out on.

Their breakup had been the start of his spiritual awakening and his decision to address his own issues. The wounds from his childhood ran deep and he was far from perfect. But with God's help, he healed one day at a time.

Samuel lifted a finger off the steering wheel and pointed toward a squat brick building. "Sheriff's office is over there." He brought the truck to a stop. "I'll call you in four or five hours, so we can update each other on our progress. Good luck."

Wyatt got out of the truck and crossed the street. He entered the building where a dark-haired female deputy stood beside a file cabinet with an open drawer.

The deputy, whose name tag read Mitchell, studied Wyatt for a moment. "You're the fed, right?"

Wyatt resisted the urge to roll his eyes. Despite their effort at blending in, something always gave them away. "Christine must have told you."

Deputy Mitchell pulled a file. "*Sheriff Norris* said you might be stopping by and that I should help you as much as I could."

At least that was encouraging. The deputy had been briefed, and Christine had laid out an expectation of cooperation. "Is Christine around?" He ran his hands through his dark hair.

"She has stepped out for a moment." Mitchell opened the file and flipped through the loose pages. "She should be back shortly."

"I'm right here."

Wyatt whirled around to see Christine standing in the doorway. The hard line of her mouth and the narrowed eyes suggested that she wasn't happy to see him. She must have known he wouldn't give up easily or she wouldn't have told the deputy about him.

Deputy Mitchell yanked her coat off the back of a chair and turned to Christine. "I've got a call about a fence dispute that has gotten ugly. If you want to hold down the fort, the two gentlemen have agreed to meet at the café across the street."

"Sure, Lisa, that will be fine." Christine took off her own coat and hung it on a rack as Lisa slipped out of the office. Her brown hair was pulled back in a ponytail, and she looked sharp in the sheriff's uniform. She picked up the file Deputy Mitchell had pulled out of the cabinet. "No luck finding the camp from the helicopter?"

Wyatt shook his head. "Not yet. Night searches allow us to look for lights in remote places. But we need to limit those. Don't want to raise suspicions. Emmett and Tyler's pictures are in every field office and resident agency in the Northwest, so he won't get far once he decides to surface. We think he'll stay hidden as long as he can, but we don't want to spook him."

She sat down at her desk and clicked on her computer. "If you like, we can look at a map together. I might be able to give you some insight into where to look."

"We can do that, but I—" Despite the difficult position he had put her in, she was trying to be helpful. "What I really need is for you to think about everything you have dealt with since you got elected. Maybe even something you noticed before you took office. Groups like this often start out benign and become radicalized because of one or two members. They might start off with vandalism of federal property or something like that." He detected the same flash of agitation in her features he had seen last night.

"I did think about it. I have the same thing to tell you this morning that I told you last night. There has not been any crime that set off alarm bells for me as being symptomatic of a buildup to domestic terrorism." She looked away from him and tapped on her keyboard. "You will recall that I was trained to know what to look for with that sort of thing."

Tension filled the air between them. She didn't like being pressed, but he needed answers. He stepped toward her desk. "One of Lansky's emails we intercepted specifically mentioned Mohler County. Roosevelt is symbolic to these guys because of what happened here ten years ago, like Ruby Ridge and Waco were for Timothy McVeigh. I thought maybe if you had a night to sleep on it, something would come to mind."

Christine flipped open the file. "I checked on what has been done to find Tyler Lansky. We never got a missing-child report. Was an AMBER Alert even issued?"

Christine had always been a competent investigator. Whatever her feelings were toward him, she was concerned about the kid. "His dad isn't going to hurt him. Tyler has been used as a ping-pong ball in a contentious divorce, but there is no indication there's been any abuse."

"Infecting your kid with violent philosophies is psychological abuse. I want to find that boy as bad as you do, but I think you are looking in the wrong place."

They weren't looking in the wrong place. She couldn't see past her loyalty to the townspeople. "I need some kind of lead. If you could just point me to a person who might know something."

"I am not aware of any extremist element around here. Most of the families that were a part of the siege ten years ago left the county in shame. But no one in town has forgotten about that boy being shot. I doubt they would trust an agent enough to tell you anything."

That truth hit him like a rock thrown against his chest. He couldn't go forward in the investigation without her. "You have a relationship with these people. They will talk to you."

Christine drew her mouth into a tight line. "I can give you full access to all our arrest records and reports." She paced across the floor to the coffeepot.

All her movements had been jerky and nervous since she'd come into the office. Though she maintained a professional demeanor, he knew her well enough to know she was upset about him showing up here. But was her irritation about the way they were running the case or about what they had been to each other ten years ago?

"Both Deputy Mitchell and I will help you with surveillance, or if you just need directions to someplace, or—" Her voice faltered when she spilled coffee on her hand. She cupped her other hand over it.

Sympathy surged through him as he bolted across the room. "Did you burn yourself? Let me see." He reached for her.

She twisted and pulled her hand out of reach. "It's nothing. I'll take care of it." She looked up at him, eyes like granite. "I'm still only going to deal in hard evidence, and I'm still telling you that I have not seen anything that makes me believe there is any kind of group around that is a threat." Her voice strained to the point of breaking. She turned her back to him.

He was beginning to think that he was the worst person to send on this assignment. There was an elephant in the room that was getting in the way of the investigation. All the hurt he had caused her ten years ago was rising up to the surface. The undercurrent of tension in her voice told him he had pushed hard enough. Regret washed through him over the man he used to be . . . for how he had treated her. He reached out to touch her shoulder, but withdrew. She was a married woman. He didn't want her to misinterpret the gesture. He softened his tone. "Guess I'll look at those records."

"Good." She turned back to face him and offered him an artificial smile. "If you like, I can set you up in the next room. I can pull all the reports for the last six months. You can read through them to your heart's content."

Though she was trying hard to sound cordial, the lines in her forehead revealed her anguish.

"I suppose that is a place to start," he said.

She wrote something on a piece of paper and handed it to him. "That's where you access the most recent files." She pointed. "If you go through that door, there's a quiet room with a computer. You can work there."

He had to be honest—no matter how hard he tried to dismiss it, who they had been to each other ten years ago was affecting how they related to each other now. "I'm sorry. I know this puts you in a difficult position."

Christine's tone softened. "It's all right. We're both just trying to do our job."

Wyatt sat down at a wooden table that had a desktop computer on it. Except for a clock, the walls were bare. The only other furniture was a row of file cabinets.

Christine closed the door a few minutes after he sat down, but he could still hear her moving around and talking on the phone.

After three hours of reading, his only conclusion was that this was a place that didn't have much crime. Mostly vandalism by teenagers and stolen farm equipment. But there was an illegal-weapons charge against a man named Angus Morrison that intrigued him.

Wyatt closed the window on the computer and rubbed his tired eyes. Considering that they thought this would be a two- or three-day assignment, this felt like a waste of time. He pushed his chair back, stood up and entered the main room.

Christine was gone, but the dark-haired deputy sat at her desk typing.

"Did you find anything that was helpful, Mr. Green?" She didn't look up from her computer.

"Nothing that stands out. I don't suppose you've noticed anything?"

"I can't tell you anything more than Sheriff Norris did. She did ask me to offer to take you anywhere you needed to go or at least give you directions. It's easy to get lost once you get out of town with no road signs." She pushed her chair back and walked toward the coffeepot.

"That's just the problem. Right now we are looking at thousands of acres of private and public land. We need a way to narrow down the possibilities. The best thing would be to ferret out someone who knows something and is ready to talk."

Deputy Mitchell shrugged. "We're not lying to you when we say we haven't seen or heard anything. Are you sure you're right about him coming up this way? Wouldn't Lansky have come into town with his little boy if he's here?"

"Not if he was being careful and didn't want to risk being spotted." He crossed his arms. "Emmett is not stupid. He knows we are looking for him. His plan is probably to lie low long enough for the intensity of the investigation to let up, then he'll take his kid somewhere we can never find him. The window of opportunity for us to find Tyler is pretty narrow."

After she poured herself a cup of coffee, Lisa sat back down in her chair. "That poor little boy. I do wish we could help." She clutched her coffee cup and stared off into space.

Even the deputy seemed a little guarded around him. Maybe if he could tear down some walls, she'd be willing to prod her memory a little harder. He rocked back and forth, toe to heel. "So, a woman sheriff and a female deputy. That's pretty forward thinking."

Color rose up in Lisa's cheeks as she sat her coffee cup down. "You mean since everyone in rural areas is backward thinking and behind the times." The deputy stood up and faced Wyatt. Her tone was slightly confrontational. "We're not as narrow-minded as you might think."

Great, Wyatt. Open mouth, insert foot. His

37

attempt at friendly conversation had had the opposite effect of what he had hoped. "I didn't mean anything by my comment. I am sure you and Christine do a great job." Did the young deputy know about the FBI disaster ten years ago? She couldn't be more than in her early twenties. Maybe she was from around here and had been a kid when the whole thing had happened.

Deputy Mitchell maintained a stiff-shouldered stance. "Christine is a good officer. She got elected by a huge majority. With all her experience and training, we're lucky to have her, and I know the extra income helps her out since Dustin died."

A lump caught in Wyatt's throat. Dustin was dead. As the shock spread through him, he struggled to keep his tone neutral. "Where did Christine go, anyway?" Confusion made it hard for him to think what he should do next. Christine wasn't under obligation to give him an update on her life, but she'd had opportunity at the farmhouse to tell him and hadn't.

"She went to drop some paperwork off over at the courthouse, and then she was going to the school for her daughter's choir program." Deputy Mitchell looked at the clock. "She should be headed up that way now. It's just two blocks over and around the corner."

The news about Dustin was like a tornado

whirling through him. He managed a casual response. "Great, I'll see if I can catch her."

Christine buttoned her light coat against the spring chill. The morning had not been very productive. She kept staring at the door and wondering what Wyatt was doing. She hated herself for not being able to free herself from thoughts about him. She'd been young and naive when she'd first met him. How could he still have an emotional hold on her?

Despite being older and wiser, all the emotions that had kept her hanging on in a dead-end relationship ten years ago had coursed through her like a dam breaking the moment she'd seen him. The way she felt around him made her afraid of losing control. There'd been an opportunity to tell him about Dustin, but she had needed the safeguard of him thinking she was still a married woman.

Christine shoved her hands in her pockets as the high school came into view. The building that housed the lower grades and Eva's kindergarten was just beyond that.

Maybe she was still feeling vulnerable. It had only been a year and a half since Dustin's accident. Wyatt had probably had twenty girlfriends in the past ten years. The man was a rascal.

It would be easy enough to just let Deputy

Mitchell assist him if he needed it. That would solve all her problems. Once Wyatt saw that the feds were looking in the wrong place, he'd be gone.

She heard footsteps behind her and glanced back. Wyatt ran to catch up with her. "Can't this wait, Wyatt? I'm on my way to see Eva's choir program."

"I'll walk with you. Just give me a minute." He reached out and gripped her arm just above the elbow. He held her in his gaze like a laser locked on a target. He opened his mouth to say something, but then closed it.

What was he struggling to say? He hadn't let go of her arm, and even through the thickness of the coat, she felt herself responding to his touch and remembering what it was like to be held by him. She managed a businesslike tone. "So did you find anything in the files that was helpful?"

"One of your reports was about confiscating a shotgun with the barrel sawed off."

His reading of the reports had been very thorough, but they didn't give the full picture. "Angus is an old man. He didn't even know that what he was doing was illegal."

"It's my only lead. Who else does he know? Who does he hang out with?"

"I had procedural obligation to file a report on Angus." A lump formed in her throat. "The Bureau researches behavior from sunup until sundown. But if you truly know someone, you know if they are capable of a crime." She planted her feet. "Don't make me point the finger of guilt at that old man."

Wyatt spoke in almost a whisper. "His activity looks suspicious. Buying weapons and altering them is suspect."

"On paper, yes, but I know Angus. I know his heart. I know his history, and that counts for something around here." She turned away from him. "I'm sorry it's not the lead you were hoping for."

A noise from the parking lot caused them both to turn. Christine saw a flash of red as Randy Stiller ran away from an older-model car. Randy had been in trouble more than once. Christine had promised Randy's mother she'd keep an eye on him. What was he up to now? "Randy, hey." The boy stopped and made eye contact. The guilty look on his face told her everything she needed to know. The kid was up to something. "Stop right there, Randy." She stepped out into the parking lot and chased after him.

She'd gone ten paces when an explosive boom surrounded her. A force of wind and heat threw her backward. Debris flew around her. Metal clattered as her body impacted with hard concrete. Everything went dark.

THREE

Even before the last piece of metal clattered to the ground, Wyatt dived into the fiery aftermath of the car bomb. He inhaled thick smoke, coughing.

He registered the fire that shot out from what remained of the car and heard the cacophony of panicked voices around him. But all of the noise and mayhem was like a radio turned down low. All he could see, all he could think about was Christine. The blast had tossed her sideways and now she lay motionless, forty feet from the burning car.

She wasn't moving. The percussive thrum of his heart beating in his ears blocked out all other sound as though he were in a tunnel that led directly to her. He ran. Feet pounding pavement. He dived to the ground beside her and felt for a pulse at her neck.

She was alive.

With his hand still cupping her cheek, he leaned closer. She looked so pale and lifeless. "Christine, can you hear me?"

No response.

Dear God, let her be okay.

He jerked back when he saw the blood soaking through the collar of her torn coat.

A hand squeezed his shoulder. "What can I do?" The voice was calm, authoritative.

He looked up into the eyes of an older man in a suit. "She needs medical attention now."

"The hospital is just down that way." The older man pointed. "I can call."

"How far is it?" He could see the two-story white building with the blue symbol for hospital over the other buildings.

"Three blocks. One down, two to the west."

"It would be faster if I took her." He lifted Christine. She was like a rag doll in his arms. He turned, finally able to absorb what was going on around him. A crowd had formed on the sidewalk not far from the burning car. "Do you work here?"

"I'm the principal of the high school. Is Christine going to be okay?"

Wyatt didn't stay around to answer the question. Holding Christine close to his chest, he ran across the lot toward the sidewalk. Without slowing his pace, he crossed the street, grateful that the hospital was clearly marked.

Christine moaned. She opened her eyes. Her gaze was unfocused.

Still running and out of breath, Wyatt looked down at her. He could lose her. So much had gone unsaid between them. "Just for the record—" he gasped for air "—I did love you. I just didn't know how to say it."

As quickly as she had opened them, her eyes

closed. He was only yards from the hospital entrance.

A woman in a nurse's smock and a man stood outside the door. When they saw Wyatt coming, they pushed a gurney toward him.

The nurse spoke. "Principal Slater phoned ahead. Put her on this, and we'll get her inside."

He laid Christine's limp body down. The medical team pushed her through the doors where a third man had come outside to hold the doors. Wyatt stepped inside, prepared to follow the gurney down the hall.

The third man gripped Wyatt's elbow, stopping him. "They need to get her stabilized. It would be better if you waited out here."

A sense of emptiness filled Wyatt as he watched the gurney disappear around a corner. "What?" He couldn't comprehend what the man was saying. All he could think about was Christine. There had been no life in her eyes when she'd looked at him. He wanted to be with her.

"I'm sorry, sir, are you a relative?"

"I'm . . . I'm . . ." Who was he to her anymore? "I'm a friend. We knew each other years ago."

"So, you're not a relative." The man scurried behind a desk and pulled forms out of file cabinets. "I know Maggie Norris. I'll give her a call. She can come in and fill out the paper-work."

Wyatt felt himself going numb as a sense of helplessness invaded his thoughts.

"Sir, why don't you have a seat? As soon as we know something, we'll let you know." The man's printer fired to life spewing out forms.

"I want to be with her." Wyatt's voice was barely above a whisper.

"I can appreciate that, but you are going to have to wait."

His heart was still jackhammering in his chest from the exertion and the adrenaline. "When will they know?"

The phone rang, and the man behind the desk gave short, quick answers and then said, "All right, I'll give Dr. Quaid a call."

Wyatt rose to his feet. "Was that about Christine?"

The man held the phone in midair as though he were debating if he should tell Wyatt or not. "It looks like she is going to need a surgeon. We don't have one on staff. This is only a twenty-bed facility."

Desperation bombarded his thoughts. "How long will that take?"

"The more you interrupt me, the longer it will take." The man's words were forceful but calm. "I can see you are concerned about her."

Wyatt backed down. Unable to sit still, he paced and waited and prayed. His breathing slowed and his heart rate returned to normal. Finally, he stumbled to the plastic waiting-room chairs and slumped down. His thoughts raced a hundred miles an hour.

What if she didn't make it?

Christine awoke in a fog . . . not sure of where she was or what had happened. She opened her eyes, but shut them quickly in reaction to the bright light. As she struggled to orient herself, a strong, warm hand squeezed hers.

"Hey, sleepyhead. There you are. How are you doing?" The voice was filled with concern.

The voice was Wyatt's. That rich tenor tone had always stirred her up inside. She turned her head, which caused pain to shoot through her shoulder. "Could you . . . could you . . . turn off those lights?"

"Sure, sure." His warm touch faded, and a moment later, she heard clicking, and the room became darker.

The sterile smells and stiff sheets told her she was in a hospital bed. Wyatt returned, scooting the chair he'd been sitting in closer to her bed.

"How long have I been out?"

"About ten hours. They had to do some minor surgery on your shoulder . . . to extract some metal. And you have a concussion."

She swallowed to produce some moisture in her mouth. "It was a bomb?"

"Yes." Without her asking, Wyatt grabbed a cup off the tray beside her bed and placed it under her mouth. "Drink this. It'll help. It's just water."

The water soothed her throat and moistened her dry mouth, bringing relief.

"Better?" He touched her forehead tenderly.

This was a side of Wyatt she had never seen before. He responded to her needs even before she voiced them.

As coherency returned, so did fear. "Eva. Where is Eva?" She lifted her head, let out an involuntary moan of pain and lay back down.

Wyatt made shushing sounds as he rubbed his knuckles over her cheek. "She and her grandma just went down the hall to get something to eat. They should be back any minute. They'll be glad to see you've come around."

"Is she doing okay with seeing me like this?"

Wyatt patted her hand. "She's handling it just fine. Your deputy has popped in a couple of times, too . . . not to mention half the town."

Christine's heart warmed. People were like that around here.

Wyatt paused. He pulled his hand away. "Christine, I know you don't want to hear this, but I sent Agent Cranson over to do a prelim investigation of the car bomb. A similar type of bomb was used in a judge's car down in Wyoming. The militia group we are after, the one Lansky is linked to, took credit for it and said next time they would make sure the judge was in it when it went off."

Christine stared at the ceiling. "It doesn't make sense that this group would set off a car bomb if they are trying to hide out at a training camp. Why would they call attention to themselves like that?"

Wyatt cleared his throat. "That's true. We are looking into the owner of the car, trying to find a motive."

Christine took in a shallow breath. "Whether there's a link or not, we need to investigate. The first thing to do would be to question Randy. He was standing by the car when I yelled at him. He might have seen something."

"You mean the kid you were running after in the parking lot? He has disappeared . . . which makes him look suspicious. Your deputy has put out an alert to all local law enforcement to be on the lookout for him."

A lot had happened in ten hours. Christine winced. Slicing pain in her shoulder made any kind of movement difficult. "Randy has had some petty-thievery problems. I doubt he knows anything about bomb making. I know his mother. Soon as I am out of here, we can go over and talk to her."

"We?"

Still resting her head on the pillow, she turned to face him. "I know you want all the dots to connect, but I am not jumping to any conclusions. If you go over there to talk to Randy's mom alone, she'll clam up. Let's face it, Green, you need me, even if you are a hotshot agent."

Wyatt grinned. "I suppose you're right about that." His expression grew more serious. "One good thing about the bomb—it gives us as agents a reason for being here without anyone thinking we are looking for that camp."

Christine tensed. "How many agents got called in? Swarms of feds descending on Roosevelt won't do anyone any good. It'll just open up old wounds."

"We've got three bomb specialists flying in, and I thought it best to use some law enforcement from a nearby county to help with the evidence gathering," Wyatt said. "A bomb blast scares people. I think we will get the cooperation we hope for."

"I hope so." She'd feel better once she could get out of this hospital bed and help facilitate the interaction between agents and townspeople. "I'll help as much as I can to ensure things go smoothly. I don't remember much of my training about bombs. It was kind of limited, and it's been a long time."

"You ever regret not using all of that training?" Wyatt fingered the wrap on his forearm.

"My priorities changed." Trying to ignore the pain radiating from her shoulder, she let out a breath. "I wanted to be on the ranch with Dustin."

As though someone had flipped a switch, Wyatt's jovial expression darkened. He rose to his feet and turned away. His shoulders slumped as a tense silence spiraled through the room.

"What is it?" she asked.

"Why didn't you tell me Dustin had died?"

So he had found out. "I . . . I just couldn't find the right moment."

"Mommy." Eva's sweet voice came from the doorway. She heard footsteps and then Eva's bright face was right next to hers. "You woke up."

She touched her daughter's soft cheek. "Yes, sweetie, I woke up."

Grandma Maggie, with her sweater folded over her forearm, came and stood at the end of the bed. "So good to see you perking up." She patted Christine's foot.

"Your family's here. I'll be going." Hurt tainted Wyatt's words.

Christine easily detected that Wyatt was upset over her not saying anything about Dustin. In the course of their relationship, she'd gotten good at reading his signals. "I'll get in touch with you as soon as I check out, and we'll go talk to Randy's mom. That seems like the best place to start."

"Your deputy can do it," he said. "She wasn't just caught in a car-bomb explosion."

His words jabbed at her heart. Was he punishing her for not saying anything about Dustin? Christine felt conflicted over the suggestion that Lisa should help Wyatt. Earlier today that had seemed like the perfect solution, but she couldn't let her personal feelings interfere with her professional judgment. Lisa was not an experienced investigator. "I'll be out of here soon enough. I want to handle this." She just hadn't been prepared for the resurgence of emotions she thought long dead. Being with him made her . . . afraid. She didn't trust herself not to fall into old patterns around him.

She couldn't discern the look on his face as he opened the hospital-room door. He left without saying another word. She listened to his footsteps fade.

Eva climbed into the bed with Christine.

"Eva, be careful." Grandma Maggie moved closer to the head of the bed.

"I want to be close to Mommy." Eva touched a bandage on Christine's forehead.

"She's all right, Maggie." She looked into her daughter's sympathy-filled eyes. "Just watch the IV, honey."

"The doctors said you can check out in the morning." Maggie turned toward the door. "Mr. Green certainly left in a hurry after he had been so worried about you."

"Really?"

Maggie moved closer to the head of the bed. "He carried you all the way to the hospital, and as soon as they would let him, he stayed by your side."

Warmth swelled around Christine's heart.

Wyatt had never been that attentive to her before, but past experience made her reluctant to trust his actions. "He probably was just waiting until you guys got back." She wasn't sure what to think about Wyatt. He had always been about work. Maybe he just thought being nice to her would help him get his assignment done faster. Still, something about him was different.

Maggie patted her hand. "You look tired. Come on, Eva, let's go home. You can see Mommy in the morning before I take you to school."

A few minutes after they left, a nurse brought in a meal for Christine. She picked at her pudding and sandwich, but was able to finish the container of milk. Christine drowsed while some mindless show played on the television. When she was still half-asleep, a nurse came in and offered her a painkiller.

She awoke in the darkness hours later. The television had been turned off. Though the curtains were drawn, she could see through a sliver between them that it was black outside. Her brain told her body to wake up, but the painkiller made that order impossible to follow. Her limbs felt heavy, immobile. She fell asleep again.

Her eyes shot open. Had an hour passed or only minutes? She was sweating and chilled at the same time. Bits and pieces of what had happened during the blast had come back to her in her dreams. A loud boom had surrounded her.

52

In her dreams, she had remembered the strength of Wyatt's arms. She had heard his frantic voice telling her she was going to be all right. His face had been very close to hers.

She'd opened her eyes for a moment. What had he said to her? *Just for the record, I did love you. I just didn't know how to say it.*

She wiped the perspiration on her brow and shivered at the same time. No, Wyatt hadn't said that to her. She had just dreamed it. Her mind was filling in the blank spaces of memory with wishful hoping.

The heaviness of sleep returned and she drifted off. When she awoke, she had no idea how much time had passed. Ten minutes? An hour? The room was dark and the view through the half-open curtain was black. The painkiller still weighted her limbs. Her mind moved in slow motion. She was shivering.

A rustling in the corner caused her to turn her head.

"Wyatt?" Her throat had gone dry.

The bulk of the figure told her it couldn't be Wyatt, but someone was in the room. Must be a doctor. Her eyelids felt heavy. The painkiller made it hard to stay awake. She pulled the covers tighter around her neck.

As she drifted off again, she heard a harsh voice. "You better watch your step with these feds, Sheeeriiiiiff."

Chilled and frightened, Christine struggled to open her eyes. The voice had been a low whisper and had come from a few feet away. She hadn't heard footsteps. Was he still here?

With her heart hammering in her chest, she reached for her call button.

A nurse appeared a few minutes later in the doorway. The dark room covered the nurse in shadow, making it hard to see her face. "Yes?"

"There was somebody in my room." Christine lifted her uninjured hand and pointed to where she'd seen movement.

"If you don't mind, I'll turn on the lights." The nurse spoke in that compassionate but noncommittal tone that medical people learned to master.

The lights went on. Christine winced from the brightness. There was nothing in the corner but her coat thrown over a chair.

The nurse tilted her head to one side and offered Christine a quick smile. She pulled a blanket out of a closet and walked over to her. She put her face close to Christine's as she smoothed out the blanket. "You must be cold."

Christine closed her eyes. The look of pity on the nurse's face was a little too much to take. She was a stable, clear-thinking adult. Why would she imagine someone was in her room? "You didn't see anyone come in here or leave?"

The nurse shook her head. "We've only got two

other patients besides you. It's real quiet. So I would notice."

"I just thought—" Now with the lights on and the nurse seeming so rational, Christine began to doubt herself.

"Don't be too hard on yourself. You've been through a lot today and everybody is affected differently by the painkillers." The nurse moved toward the door. "Would you like the lights out?"

"No, please, leave them on." Real or imagined, Christine didn't want to face what waited for her in the dark.

FOUR

"Aren't we a pair?" Wyatt commented as he entered the sheriff's office. He pointed to the wrap he wore on his injured arm and then to Christine's bandaged shoulder. She looked pretty good considering she'd had minor surgery the day before. She'd left her long brown hair loose, which intensified the rich brown of her eyes.

A positive charge passed between them when she smiled in agreement. "We are both pretty beat up."

She'd called only an hour before and said she was feeling well enough to conduct the interview with Randy's mother. Deputy Mitchell had had a long night following leads on Randy's whereabouts, none of which had panned out. She wouldn't be on duty until later.

Any renewed attraction he felt should have been doused by the roadblocks she'd put up indicating she only wanted their time together to be about work, but it hadn't. That he found himself longing to see that look of adoration in her eyes like he'd seen ten years ago didn't make any sense. He was a glutton for punishment.

Christine grabbed her coat off the back of a chair. She winced, obviously in pain.

He rushed over to her. "It's going to be hard to lift your arm. Let me help you get that coat on."

"Thank you." Both her voice and her eyes welcomed the offer.

She hadn't rebuffed him like she had when she'd burned her hand. The smallest positive response from her gave him hope. He still didn't know why she had kept Dustin's death from him. Maybe later she would explain.

As he eased the coat over her injured shoulder, his fingers grazed the silken skin of her neck. She let out a breath and then turned and looked at him, warmth filling her eyes.

"Did I hurt you?"

"No, I—" Her voice lilted up.

Without thinking, he reached up and pulled her hair free from the coat collar. He found himself wanting to linger close enough to be enveloped by the scent of her perfume.

She turned away from him; her movements were jerky as she picked up her purse. "We should get going." She clipped her words. Her body language, her voice, it all indicated that he had stepped over a boundary. But he had seen a flash of something in her eyes, a moment of vulnerability.

"How's your shoulder? Are you up to driving?"

"Actually, it hurts when I lift it higher than a couple of inches." She handed him the keys.

They got in the SUV that had the word *Sheriff* on the door with Wyatt behind the wheel. Christine gave him directions. It only took a few minutes to get to the trailer park where Randy's mother lived. With few exceptions, most of the trailers looked well maintained. The yards were uncluttered with the green grass of spring just beginning to overtake the brown patches.

Christine went up the steps and knocked on the door. "She knows we're coming. I called her earlier."

The door opened and a redheaded woman who looked as if she was barely out of her twenties opened the door. She leaned toward Christine, offering her a soft smile before she looked Wyatt up and down with suspicion. Christine was right about one thing. There was no way he could conduct this investigation without her.

"Vicki, how are you doing?"

"I'm holding up all right, considering." If she was as young as she looked, Vicki must have had Randy when she was a teenager. "Your deputy came by earlier." Worry crinkled her forehead and she wrapped the cardigan she was wearing tighter around her torso. "Still no sign of Randy."

Christine placed a supportive hand on Vicki's shoulder. "May we come in?"

Vicki stepped to one side. Shag carpet and earth-tone wallpaper dated the tidy living room. An old man hooked up to an oxygen tank sat watching television. "I don't know what else I can tell you that the deputy hasn't already asked," Vicki said.

Vicki seemed to think the purpose for them coming by was to find Randy, not to find out if he was connected with the bomb blast. Christine hadn't said anything to make her think otherwise.

Wyatt spoke up. "He hasn't tried to contact you?"

Vicki shook her head. The flush of color in her pale cheeks indicated that the ordeal had been gut-wrenching for her. "I don't know what I am going to do with that boy."

Wyatt pulled out a notebook. His partner, Cranson, had briefed him on what they had discovered so far about the bombing. "Randy was last seen running away from a car that was registered to Daniel Hart."

"You mean the car that exploded." Vicki massaged her neck. "Mr. Hart was Randy's history teacher. They weren't getting along. Randy thought the grades were unfair." She took in a shaky breath, obviously upset.

Christine's voice filled with sympathy. "Maybe if we looked in his room, it would give us some kind of clue as to where he has gone."

Again Vicki cast a suspicious glance toward Wyatt. "Just because my son wasn't getting along with a teacher doesn't mean he put a bomb in that car."

Christine nodded. "I know Randy has been in trouble before . . . but that doesn't make him guilty this time. Let's assume the best until we have evidence that contradicts that." The compassion in Christine's voice seemed to relax Vicki.

"Go ahead and look in his room. I doubt you will find anything." Vicki tilted her head toward the old man in the living room. "I got to lay out Dad's medication for him before I go to work."

Christine led the way down the narrow hallway past a bathroom and into a room whose posters, skateboard and general clutter indicated it belonged to a teenager.

Once they were alone, Wyatt said, "Maybe you should just conduct this investigation and report back to me." A hint of sarcasm colored his words.

"I've lived here for ten years, Wyatt. They trust me."

Wyatt and Christine wandered around the

room. He scanned the collection of CDs while Christine lifted a pile of what looked like school papers on a cluttered desk. Wyatt pushed open the folding closet door and kneeled down. Several books were pushed toward the back of the closet and partially covered with a T-shirt. Wyatt pulled the books out.

Christine lifted a skateboard away from the wall where it was propped up before looking at Wyatt. "He's got a bookshelf over there. Why keep books in his closet?"

"Because these—" Wyatt held up a book titled *Anarchy for Amateurs* "—are probably the ones he doesn't want anyone to know he is reading." The other book was on the second amendment and gun rights and looked as if it had been self-published.

"It still doesn't mean anything, Wyatt. Kids are sometimes just curious about things they know they shouldn't get into." Christine's gaze landed on a series of photographs on a shelf.

Wyatt put the books back where he had found them.

Just as Christine picked up one of the framed pictures, Vicki appeared in the doorway. "That's Randy with his favorite teacher, Mr. Champlain. He also coached basketball. He took Randy to quite a few basketball camps."

Christine's expression changed as she slowly put the photo back on the shelf. Was that fear he saw etched across her features . . . or something else?

Wyatt turned toward Vicki. "Your son didn't have a computer?" Wyatt wandered over to the photo wondering what had set alarm bells off for Christine. The picture was of Randy holding a basketball. Mr. Champlain, dressed in a sweat suit with a whistle around his neck, stood beside the boy.

"We can't afford a computer." Vicki shook her head. "He just used the one at school. He always took his cell phone with him, so I doubt you'll find that."

"Was there any indication that he might have come back here to get some things?"

Vicki shrugged. "I work over at the café during the day. Dad sleeps quite a bit, but he's here all the time. If Randy did come back, he must have been awful quiet."

"We'll do our best to find him," Christine said. "I know Deputy Mitchell has already tracked down anyone in town who might have known of his whereabouts or be hiding him. Does he know anyone in another town or even out of state?"

Vicki shook her head. "I can't think of who it would be. All of his cousins live close by." Vicki checked her watch. "If you don't mind, I have to get ready for work."

Christine thanked Vicki for her time, and she and Wyatt headed down the hallway to the living room. Once they were in the SUV, Wyatt said, "Are you going to tell me what that look was about?"

"What look?"

"That photo of Randy with his teacher and basketball coach. Your expression changed."

Christine pressed her lips together and took in such a deep breath that her chest visibly moved up and down. "That teacher Randy was so fond of is a respected part of this community. But I know it's a lead. As a law-enforcement officer, I have to tell you."

He could see how this was tearing her apart.

"I'm not naive," she continued. "I know that everyone in this town isn't honest and good. It's just that the good guys do look and act exactly like the bad guys . . . until they break the law. I don't want to destroy the trust that people have in me. You get to walk away from here once you find that kid. I go to church with these people. They greet me in the grocery store."

"I'll do everything in my power to protect what you have built here," he said.

Christine drew in a breath and squared her shoulders as though preparing herself for what she had to say. "This could be nothing. But several months ago, Mr. Champlain told everyone in town that he was headed down to some kind of teaching workshop in Colorado during a school holiday. That Saturday I had some business in

Placerville about twelve miles up the road. I saw Mr. Champlain coming out of a gas station. His vehicle looked like it was outfitted for a weekend of camping."

Wyatt didn't remember seeing a town named Placerville. It might just be such a bump in the road, he hadn't even noticed on a map. "What about the encounter struck you as strange?"

"It would have been no big deal. He could have just changed his plans, but then he saw me. The look on his face was filled with guilt, and he didn't wave or anything, just ducked behind his car. It was such a nonevent, I barely remembered it until I saw that photograph and realized he had a link to Randy."

Wyatt nodded. "So I guess our next step is to talk to Mr. Champlain."

Christine bristled. She didn't know Matthew Champlain except in passing. She had no reason to believe he was anything but a good teacher and a good citizen. "That does seem like the logical next step. If we kept the questioning centered on Randy's whereabouts . . ."

Wyatt shifted in his seat. "I see what you mean. We're not going to get the answers we want without raising suspicions, and if he's connected to Emmett Lansky, he could warn him."

They needed to be cautious about their next move. "There's a school holiday coming up, a three-day weekend. If Matthew Champlain is connected, he might be heading out to the camp. Maybe that is where Randy has disappeared to, too."

"Are you suggesting some kind of surveillance?"

"If nothing turns up before then, we'll just follow him . . . see where he goes. My deputy and I can rotate shifts with you and your partner."

Wyatt pulled out onto the road. "It would be best to have an agency person on each shift."

"Good, you and Deputy Mitchell can take the first shift."

Wyatt didn't answer right away. "You're the one with the surveillance training. If he is going to go anywhere, it is probably going to be the first day of break. You and I should take that shift."

Christine didn't want to read anything into Wyatt's scrambling to be on surveillance with her. She'd spent the whole of their relationship trying to read into the choices he made. He'd given a sound professional reason for them to work together. It was just that she had heard a little hitch in his voice when she had suggested Mitchell do the surveillance with him. "We've got a day. I'll see what we can set up in terms of not being detected. Maybe there's an empty house in Champlain's neighborhood. I'll look into getting a car that no one will associate with the sheriff's department or me."

"In the meantime, we've already started to run a check on Daniel Hart—the guy whose car was blown up. We can start seeing what kind of connection this Champlain guy has." Wyatt hit the blinker to turn into the sheriff's office. "It's nice to have some kind of lead."

They both knew the connection was tenuous, but it was something. "We can't afford more than a couple days of watching him. I don't exactly have a large police force at my disposal."

After bringing the car to a stop, Wyatt turned to face her, studying her with intense dark brown eyes. "I understand." He pushed the car door open. "Thanks for the help." He offered her his charming smile before stepping onto the gravel lot of her office.

By the time she opened her door and headed up the walkway, Wyatt had pulled his ringing cell phone out of his pocket.

A simple check of Champlain's address in the phone book told her that he lived out of town. She hoped there was some inconspicuous place they could watch his house from.

Wyatt poked his head back in the office door, his expression serious. "That was the forensics lab. They found Randy's prints on what was left of the explosive device. Kid's been in trouble with the law before, so he was in the system."

Christine's limbs went slack as her stomach somersaulted. "I guess that gives you the connection you were looking for. Randy is linked to the bomb and the bomb is similar to one used in Wyoming, which was the work of the group Emmett had connections to."

Wyatt said, "This might not have been the news you wanted."

"It doesn't matter what I wanted. The evidence is what it is. Clearly there is a subversive element in Roosevelt and they are teaching young boys how to build bombs." She walked over to the window and stared at the street outside as people bustled by. "The good guys *do* look exactly like the bad guys. Now I don't know who to trust or suspect."

FIVE

Uneasiness invaded Christine's thoughts as she watched two teenagers walk past the sheriff's office followed by Clarence, a retired rancher who spent most of his day at the library and the café, and a middle-aged man in a suit and cowboy hat. Anyone of them could be a member of this radicalized militia group. Her world filled with uncertainty. She thought she knew these people. She didn't feel safe in her town anymore.

"You can trust me." Wyatt placed a supportive hand on Christine's uninjured shoulder.

The warmth of Wyatt's touch permeated the layers of clothes. More than anything, she wanted to be enveloped in the protection of his arms. When she turned to face him, the look in his eyes invited her into a hug, but she couldn't do that. She had to remind herself that anyone could be attentive for a few days. Wyatt was still Wyatt and she had no desire to revisit the pain he had caused years ago.

"You look tired," he whispered.

She turned away from him. "I think I am still worn-out from yesterday." She rubbed her forehead as the pain in her shoulder became more acute. "I've got a part-time deputy coming on duty. He's retired, but he takes up the slack for Deputy Mitchell and me when needed."

"I'm sure he can handle things," Wyatt said. "I'll drive you back to your place."

"Thanks for being my chauffeur. It should only take a couple of days for it to get easier to lift my arm." Once the deputy showed up, Christine and Wyatt headed out to Wyatt's truck.

As they drove through the town, she felt as if she was seeing it with new eyes. True, there were people here who were an unwelcome element. But as she watched a young mom placing her baby into a stroller, she realized that most of the residents were the same good people she'd fallen in love with. She'd sworn to protect them, and she would do everything she could to make sure that happened.

Her mind whirled with all the information they had to process. "I still say the bombing was not supposed to happen or it has nothing to do with this group. The group hasn't taken credit for it like they did in Wyoming. And it's not logical that they would do anything to make us think they were here if they want to keep the camp and Emmett a secret."

Wyatt nodded. "Let's just assume that Randy misused his newfound knowledge for bomb making to get revenge on a teacher he was mad at, a very teenager thing to do."

"Is it possible Randy learned how to make the bomb from the internet or one of his books? That it's not connected at all to this group?"

Wyatt shook his head. "The signature for the bombs is identical, though the second one is cruder."

"If we could just find Randy, I think a lot of our questions would be answered." As they came to the edge of town, Christine turned to face Wyatt. "You were right. There is something going on if teenagers are learning how to build bombs in this town. I guess I owe you an apology."

Wyatt shook his head then reached over and patted her leg. "Don't worry about it. No one wants to believe that there is a subversive and potentially violent element in their community."

The drive out to her ranch went by quickly.

Even with its worn roof and peeling paint, the seventy-year-old farmhouse was a comforting sight. Cattle lulling in a nearby field and Maggie's freshly plowed garden patch only added to the sense of peace she felt when she was out here.

"Looks like you got company." Wyatt pointed to a battered green truck by the equipment barn.

"That's just Larry Myers. He's leasing out some of my fields to grow barley. He pays for some of the lease in labor, and we'll split the profit from the crop."

A man with a scowl on his face came out of the barn and made his way to a corral.

"So he just gets the run of the place." Wyatt's voice filled with suspicion.

She appreciated Wyatt being concerned about her safety. "Larry's all right. He works hard and has farmed his whole life. The land has to make money for us somehow. Dustin taught me quite a bit, but I can't run the whole operation by myself."

Christine wrapped her hand around the door handle. Eva was at school and Maggie had gone into town for the day. The news about Randy's fingerprints was still tumbling through her brain. She really didn't want to be alone just yet. "You want to come in for a cup of coffee? I have a map we can look at. I'll show you the little town where I saw Champlain."

• • •

While Christine put the coffee together in the kitchen, Wyatt wandered around the living room. He studied the pictures of Christine with Eva and Maggie. There was a photograph of Dustin in a hunter's vest with his arms around another man and a picture of Eva in a ballerina costume standing next to the border collie who also sported a tutu. The story of a family.

He had no idea what it meant to be a part of a family. The first sense of belonging he had was when he had joined the marines. He had no idea what it meant to live in one place for more than nine months. His mother had moved every time she had a new job or a new boyfriend. He touched the photo of Christine with Eva.

Christine entered the living room holding two steaming mugs, and Wyatt pulled his hand away from the photo. No need for her to see him getting sentimental.

Her brown hair fell around her face in soft curls and her eyes were bright. "Did you have a chance to look at the map?"

"Not yet."

She handed him the cup of coffee and turned her attention to the map she had laid out on the coffee table. "Show me where you guys have already looked."

Wyatt's shoulder touched Christine's as they bent over to study the map. He was keenly aware of the rain-washed scent of her hair.

Christine pointed out possibilities for where the camp might be. "This map shows which land is private and which is federal."

Wyatt studied the map for a moment. "I know we have looked in some of those areas."

"And this . . ." Christine ran her finger along a red line and stopped at a tiny indiscernible word. "This is Placerville—where I saw Champlain when he was supposed to be in Colorado."

Wyatt leaned closer to the map. "It must be a really small place."

"It's mostly a supply station for hunters who are heading into the deep wilderness. There's a store there with a little restaurant attached and a few homes."

Wyatt studied the map. "Looks like there are three roads that lead out from there, all of them into remote areas." Wyatt straightened up and stretched. "I've got to get back to town. I'll let you know if anything more pops up with the bombing." He tapped his finger on the map by Placerville. "We'll send the choppers out that way and maybe go out there and have a look."

Christine took a sip of coffee. "A lot has happened in the last couple of days. I'm glad you were here. I couldn't have handled the bombing and everything alone." Her lips parted as she looked up at him with wide brown eyes.

Had he detected a note of affection in her voice? "Yeah."

She stepped toward him. "Probably just routine for you."

"You know Bureau work is mostly brain work with a little bit of excitement thrown in. Do you ever think about . . ."

"Think about what?"

He wanted to ask her if she ever thought about what their life might have been like if they had stayed together, but instead he said, "If you hadn't left the Bureau."

"You keep asking me that," she said. "I like the slower pace here and one bomb blast in a lifetime is enough to deal with."

She was standing so close that it would have been nothing for him to lean in and kiss her. His heart racing, he turned away and grabbed his mug, gulping his coffee. "Stay in touch. I'll let you know if we need any support."

Christine looked a bit stunned at his abrupt exit. "Oh . . . okay . . . sure."

As he headed out to the truck, Christine came and leaned against the doorway still holding her coffee cup. She waved at him when he backed out of the driveway.

He caught a glimpse of her in his rearview mirror as she made her way across the yard to the barn. The confident stride and long hair flowing in the wind made her look vibrant. This was her home now. These were her people. As the farmhouse faded in the distance, an ache entered his heart for what might have been.

Christine shaded her eyes and watched Wyatt drive away. Something about him was different. She had seen none of the impatience that had characterized his personality ten years ago. He was tender and attentive. Maybe he had changed.

She made her way toward the barn with Jake trailing behind her. Of course, everyone mellowed with age. She'd just have to wait and see if all these changes she saw were really who he was.

She pushed open the barn door. Larry came out from behind a tractor holding a large wrench. "See you had a ride home. How's that shoulder treating you?"

By now, the whole town had heard about the bomb blast.

"I'm afraid it is making me more tired than I expected. I'm going to try to get a nap before I meet Maggie and Eva for Thursday-evening services at church."

Though his leathery skin aged him, Larry was only a few years older than she was. Outside of the time he spent on the ranch, she didn't see him much. They didn't run in the same circles. Most of Larry's social life revolved around hunting and drinking.

Larry twirled the wrench and made his way

over to a combine. "Got to get this equipment running before the seed goes in."

Christine tensed. "Is fixing it going to cost a lot? I just assumed everything was working okay."

A fire came into his eyes and he set his jaw. "Having running equipment has to be part of the deal. I can't put the seed in by hand." Larry tossed the wrench on the ground.

They hadn't talked about equipment repair when they had worked out their deal. Christine held up a hand as if that would stop the rising tide of anger. "Just let me know before you spend any money on parts. I understand about working equipment, but I have to be careful about how much money I spend."

The first planting season after Dustin had died she had not had the energy to do anything. It had only taken a year of the bills piling up to make her realize she either had to sell the ranch or make it pay for itself. She'd thought that Larry was the answer to her problems.

Larry shook his head, picked up the wrench and turned his back, loosening a bolt on the combine. His stiff, quick motions told her that he was still upset.

Genuinely conciliatory, Christine moved toward him. "I suppose we should have considered details like that when we signed that agreement."

Larry tossed his wrench into the toolbox. The clatter of metal against metal filled the barn.

"We'll figure it out." He wiped his brow on his forearm and spat on the ground. "Kind of stretches you thin to be the sheriff and run this ranch, doesn't it?"

"I'm doing okay." It seemed an odd thing to say since most ranchers worked a second job.

"That guy you pulled up with is a fed, isn't he?"

"He's here to investigate the bombing." Christine nodded and shoved her hands in her pockets, not sure where Larry was leading with his questions.

"I'm sure he's only increased your workload." Larry pulled a grease rag out of his back pocket and wiped his hands. "You want my advice, Ms. Norris? Nothing good comes out of working with the feds."

"I'm the sheriff. I don't have a lot of choice in the matter." Her voice softened. "Most of the time the FBI does a good job."

Larry raised his eyebrows and his words had a sarcastic edge to them. "Most of the time."

The siege and the teenager's death didn't need to be mentioned specifically for them both to know what they were talking about.

Larry turned his attention to a carburetor on a piece of plywood. "Just better be careful." He straightened his posture and looked directly at her. "That's all I'm saying."

He stared at her for a moment longer as his words hung in the air.

Christine took a step back. "Let me know if you end up needing to buy parts." She made her way toward the barn door. Dry hay crunched beneath her feet. Larry had never been one for conversation and pleasantries. His work ethic and his expertise made up for his lack of communication skills.

Up until now, Larry's lack of social graces hadn't bothered her. But something about their conversation made her uneasy. As she made her way back to the house, she couldn't help but feel that something in what Larry had said felt vaguely like a threat.

SIX

"Oh, look who has come to church." Grandma Maggie touched Christine's arm above the elbow and pointed to where Wyatt stood across the church foyer.

Christine waited outside the Sunday-school room where she had just dropped Eva off. The midweek crowd shuffled through the wide doors of the church. Across two rows of pews, Mrs. Blevenger had cornered Wyatt. He bent forward to listen to what the short, elderly woman said while she patted his hand. He'd exchanged his T-shirt and jeans for a pair of khakis and a crisp, white button-down shirt. Christine's breath caught in her throat. Church was the last place she had ever expected to see Wyatt.

As Mrs. Blevenger shuffled away, Wyatt raised his head and scanned the room. Christine felt a charge of electricity when his gaze rested on her.

"You should ask him to sit with us. I'm sure he doesn't know anybody," Maggie said.

Uncertain of Wyatt's motive for showing up, Christine dug in her heels. "Oh, Maggie, I don't think we need to do that."

Maggie squeezed Christine's arm. Her voice dropped into a whisper. "I miss Dustin as much as you do, but it has been a year and a half. Go on, now."

"I don't know if that is such a good idea. Maggie, I didn't just meet Agent Green a couple of days ago . . . We knew each other when I was with the Bureau. We have . . . a history."

Maggie rebuffed Christine's resistance with a wave of her hand. "You are just sitting together in church. It's the friendly thing to do."

Christine drew her lips into a tight line. God had been the furthest thing from Wyatt's mind when they had been together. Had he actually changed or was there something else going on?

Wyatt wove through the crowd entering the church and stood beside Christine. Maggie poked her in the back.

"Nice to see you here." Christine swallowed as

her mouth went dry. "Do you have a place to sit?"

He shook his head, his dark eyes sparkling like onyx. His black hair was slicked back and he'd gotten rid of his five-o'clock shadow. One thing was for sure. Wyatt Green had never been short on charisma or good looks. But was there something deeper to him now?

"We usually sit over there in the middle," Maggie jumped in.

"After you, ladies." Wyatt swept his arm forward.

Maggie hustled ahead and chose a spot in the middle of the pew, which meant Christine would sit beside Wyatt. When he settled in a few inches from her, she was aware of his proximity, tuned in to every move that he made.

There were two other churches in town. Why had he picked this one?

Wyatt was a trained investigator. From Eva's Sunday school pictures on the refrigerator to old church bulletins lying around the house, it wouldn't have been hard for him to figure out which church they attended.

In the lull before service officially began, she leaned close to him and whispered, "You're full of surprises."

He arched an eyebrow. "Am I?"

"When did your feelings about God change?"

He opened his mouth to answer, but the hush of the congregation and the minister moving to the podium made answering her question disruptive. She'd just have to wait.

The choir burst into song and Christine focused on the words of worship on the overhead.

The back of his hand brushed against hers when they stood up to sing a hymn. He smiled, and her legs turned into cooked noodles.

Christine sat through the sermon with her fingers laced together. When she looked over at Wyatt, he was nodding in agreement to what the pastor said. His interest seemed to be genuine.

Even as she felt her heart opening to him, she knew she needed to be cautious.

Maggie leaned close and whispered in her ear, "We should have him out to dinner after service."

Christine responded with a stern look as old fears returned. Nothing here needed to be rushed. There was a wall somewhere in her heart that she had built up against ever again feeling the kind of pain Wyatt had caused. And now here was the source of all those hard lessons sitting beside her. She wanted to believe that he was different, but only a fool put her hand on a hot burner twice.

The minister's comments indicated that he was nearing the end of his service.

Wyatt's phone must have vibrated because he drew it out of his pocket and checked the message. His eyebrows furled as he read, concern etched across his face. He leaned toward her and whispered, "I gotta go. Something has come up.

I'll let you know if it's important." He patted her hand and slipped out of the bench so quietly that no one even turned in his direction.

Christine sat as the choir sang their closing number. The memory of his touch on her hand, of his breath warming her ear, lingered.

She slipped quietly out of the bench and raced to the door as the other parishioners were gathering together coats and Bibles and children.

The cold spring air hit her when she rushed outside, forming goose bumps on her arms. She scanned the parking lot just in time to see Wyatt pulling out of the far end. She crossed her arms against the chilly spring wind and wondered what could have been so urgent as to pull him out of the service early.

Wyatt eased onto the highway heading toward the motel where he and Agent Cranson had set up headquarters, just outside of town. Questions raced through his mind, and he struggled to stay under the speed limit. Cranson's text message had been rather cryptic: come now, big break.

He regretted having to leave early. He had intended to go to a service while he was in town, but had picked Christine's church on purpose. Though Christine's indifference to him was not what he had hoped for, he understood it. She still didn't trust him. Maybe they could have talked after the service about Dustin . . . about other things. Would he have been able to share all the changes that happened since they had broken up or would he have clammed up?

He pulled into the gravel lot by the motel. Cranson stood outside the room waiting for him. His stiff posture and furled eyebrows were disconcerting. Calling something a big break usually meant it was good news for the investigation.

Wyatt slammed the truck door. "Have they located Emmett?"

"If only it were that easy." Cranson shook his head and turned back toward the motel room. Inside, they had set up a makeshift office. "There was a bank robbery in Idaho." Cranson picked up a file of papers. "The perpetrators are still at large, but the surveillance cameras took a few pictures."

Wyatt read the details of the robbery and then filed through the pictures. He studied the first two; neither man looked familiar.

Cranson tapped on the second picture. "That guy has an arrest record, and we've linked him to Emmett and his group. The robbery is the start of the escalation, to finance their movement."

None of this was good. No wonder Cranson had had that worried look on his face. Wyatt studied the next picture. The third guy he might have seen in some file, but the fourth picture knocked the wind out of him. Surveillance photos were grainy at best, but this one caught the perpetrator looking right at the camera. "It's the missing kid, Randy Stiller."

"He probably had out-of-state connections to the group, hitchhiked into Idaho and someone introduced him to the fine art of robbing banks for a cause." Cranson ran his fingers through his graying hair.

Wyatt shook his head. "He's just a kid." Any hope that Randy had not connected with a subversive element was gone. "What about his teacher, Matthew Champlain?"

"No link to any of the known members of this group, but Champlain *has* posted some things online that match up with their antigovernment, 'violence-is-the-solution' belief system," Cranson said.

So it was possible Champlain was responsible for Randy's messed-up worldview. Randy certainly was ripe for the picking with a group like this, a troubled teen looking for a father figure. Wyatt filed through the photos again. Something about the third man bugged him. "I've seen this guy recently."

"I can tell you where we've seen him before," Cranson responded. "You know the file we have on this militia group is four inches thick." He walked back over to the dresser where stacks of documents were piled. "I printed this one out because I remembered it from the file. You'll see why right away."

Wyatt studied the photograph. Taken three weeks ago, it showed Emmett Lansky and the third bank robber coming out of a restaurant in Colorado.

"Emmett and this guy, whoever he is, are linked," Cranson said.

Wyatt shook his head as he studied the photo. "No, I've seen him even more recently than this."

"There's more news." Cranson sat on the end of the hotel bed. The expression on his face was grim. "The Bureau isn't happy with our progress here. Because of this robbery, they've widened the search, put some teams in Idaho among other states. If we don't come up with something in the next couple of days, they're going to pull us out."

"Lansky's ex said he was making frequent trips up to this area," Wyatt said. "I just know we are in the right place."

"But Lansky has connections all over the Northwest. Maybe he didn't come here because he knew it was the first place we'd look."

Wyatt spread the pictures out on the dresser, focusing on the third suspect. Where had he seen that guy? It was in another photograph some-where. Mentally, he went through a catalog of every place he had been since he had arrived in Roosevelt. The photographs that people put on display were of people and events that mattered to them. Something sparked in his mind.

He'd seen this man in a photograph on

Christine's mantel. The man who was now implicated in a robbery had had his arm around Dustin.

The knock on the door took Christine by surprise. She rose from the abundant dinner that she and Maggie had prepared as part of their after-church routine. She glanced out the window. Wyatt's truck was parked outside.

She opened the door.

"Christine, there have been some developments in the case."

The worried look on his face told her the "developments" had to do with Roosevelt. "It'll have to wait until after dinner. You can join us, but I don't want Maggie and Eva having to sit through our shoptalk."

"I understand," he said.

She walked back toward the kitchen, talking over her shoulder. "Is that what that text message in church was about?"

"Yeah, sorry about leaving service early." Wyatt hesitated at the fireplace, staring at the photographs. His features darkened for a moment.

"We're in the kitchen," Christine said. He certainly looked at those photographs a lot. In the whole time they had been together, Wyatt had never gone to visit any relatives nor had any come to visit him. Maybe seeing pictures of a family stirred up some kind of longing in him. Mentally,

84

Christine kicked herself. She was doing it again. Trying to read something into each subtle change in his expression because he would never just come out and tell her what he was feeling.

The dinner conversation centered around the preparations Maggie needed to get done to get her garden ready for spring planting, and Eva's ballet recital.

"Been a long time since I had a home-cooked meal." He poured the gravy over his second helping of roast beef and mashed potatoes.

Eva wiggled in her seat and pounded her spoon on the center of her potatoes. "Mama likes to cook."

"It's always nicer when you have someone to cook for, though." Maggie looked directly at Christine and raised her eyebrows.

Christine resisted the urge to kick the older woman in the shins. "I don't have that much time to cook anymore, since I took on the sheriff duties."

Wyatt shoveled a forkful of potatoes in his mouth. "Too bad, this is really good."

She had to admit there had always been something very satisfying about cooking a meal and having a man sing its praises.

Eva waved her spoon in the air. "Mama's going to get me a purple dress for my dance recital."

"You'll be the prettiest girl there," Wyatt said.

Wyatt's compliment caused Eva to smile, revealing a row of pearl-like teeth. She clasped her hands together and angled from side to side in her chair, leaning a little closer to Wyatt.

Wyatt whispered something in Eva's ear that made her laugh.

Christine stiffened and took in a sharp breath. Though Eva seemed drawn to him, Christine didn't want Eva forming an attachment to Wyatt. He'd exit their lives as quickly as he entered. She was only five, she didn't need any more loss in her life.

Christine waited until Wyatt finished his last bite. "Maggie, Wyatt came by because he has some work-related developments to discuss with me."

"I can clean up the kitchen and watch Eva." Maggie rose from the table and picked up a dish. "I'll bring you two some cobbler in just a little bit."

Christine ushered Wyatt into the living room. He paced the carpet seeming to struggle with what he had to say. Twice he glanced at Christine and then at the photos on the mantel.

"So spill it," she said. "What's the development?"

"The FBI is widening their search for Emmett. If we don't come up with something solid in the next couple of days, the agent in charge is going to pull us out and assign us elsewhere."

Christine felt a stab to her heart. Wyatt would be leaving sooner than she thought. A day ago, she would have been grateful for the departure. Now she wasn't so sure. He had a newfound faith, and she'd seen signs that he was a different man than he had been ten years ago. "I suppose you've got to follow orders. I don't know what else I can do to shake the bushes. Hopefully, following Champlain will turn up something. You will stay for that, won't you?"

Wyatt nodded and ran his hands through his hair then rubbed his chin. He hesitated before speaking again. "The big break is that we know what happened to Randy."

Something in his tone told her it wasn't good news. "Am I going to have to tell his mother something she doesn't want to hear?"

"He's alive, but he's a suspect in a robbery in Idaho, and he's still at large."

Christine let out a breath. "Vicki will be devastated. She works so hard to scrape together a life for herself and that boy. She's got her hands full with taking care of her father. I just so wanted things to be okay with her kid. I'll be the one to let her know."

Wyatt's pacing stopped in front of the fireplace mantel again. He shoved his hands in his pockets and tilted his head toward one of the photographs. "Who's the guy in the photo with Dustin?"

Christine didn't quite follow the logic of his line of questioning. She moved beside him and picked up the photograph. "That's Harrison Van Norman. He was one of Dustin's hunting buddies."

She hadn't looked at the photograph in a long time. Dustin's smile still warmed her heart.

"He's not around here anymore?"

"No, he left shortly after Dustin died." She hadn't thought about Harrison much. That time of her life was still a grief-filled fog. The memories were unclear. He had come by a few times after Dustin died and been very kind. "I'm not even sure where he went."

"How well did Dustin know him?"

Christine took a step back. "Why are you asking all these questions about Harrison . . . and Dustin?" She wasn't sure she wanted to hear the answer.

Angst clouded Wyatt's features. "Harrison was one of the other suspects in the robbery."

Her breath caught. Harrison had been a frequent visitor to their house. She had thought of him as a friend. "Are you sure?"

"I can show you the surveillance photo."

"He was Dustin's good friend." Christine pressed the photo frame to her chest as a realization spread through her. "You don't think Dustin had anything to do with all of this?"

"That's not what I was saying. These are just questions that I have to ask."

Christine felt her defenses going up. "I don't agree with your line of questioning. Dustin died over a year ago. I think your personal feelings are interfering with your professional judgment."

Anger flashed momentarily across his face, but his answer was calm. "What are you talking about?"

"My husband was a good man."

"I never said he wasn't. I just wanted to know what his association was with Harrison. You've got the guy's picture on your mantel. You must have been close to him." Wyatt spoke slowly, as though he was choosing his words carefully.

Christine felt as if the carpet had been pulled out from under her life. He was asking her to revise her past . . . to rethink what she knew about Dustin's friends. "Harrison was over at the house all the time. I thought I knew what kind of man he was." Unable to process all that Wyatt was implying, she turned her back.

Wyatt circled around so he could look at her. "Are you telling me you didn't know about this side of Harrison's life? Maybe Dustin suspected something and told you. That's why I am asking you these questions. My intent is not to cast a shadow on Dustin. But if they were as close as you say they were, he might have known something."

Maggie appeared in the doorway. "My, my, things are getting a little loud in here. Maybe some cobbler would help calm you two down." Maggie placed the bowl in Christine's hands and then handed the other bowl to Wyatt. "I'll leave you two to it."

Christine couldn't help the steely glare she gave Wyatt. What was he doing stirring things up about the past, opening a door that made her feel the grief all over again? She still hadn't recovered from learning that Harrison wasn't the man she thought he was. She couldn't get past the ïdea that Wyatt's judgment was clouded when it came to Dustin. If Dustin had known anything, he would have brought it to the attention of the law even if Harrison was his friend. "It's possible that Harrison adopted an extremist philosophy after Dustin died."

"Anything is possible, but you know from profiling that most people hold radical ideas for years before they work up to acting on them. This guy Harrison just acted on them."

Christine's shoulders dropped, and she softened her defensive stance. He was right about that. "I just don't know what to think right now."

He placed the bowl of cobbler on the mantel. "I'm not very hungry anymore. I'll go." He treaded to the door and eased it open. "Just for the record, Christine. I never let my personal feelings interfere with my job." He closed the door softly.

She listened to Wyatt's truck revving to life, so stirred up inside that she couldn't bring herself to sit down or take a deep breath. Dustin and Harrison had been close. There were only two options. If it didn't make sense that Harrison's radical views had led to illegal activity in a year's time, the most likely scenario was that Dustin knew about Harrison's leanings, continued to be friends with him and remained silent. Or worse, that he had agreed with Harrison's ideas. What did that say about her late husband?

She crossed her arms and wandered to the window. Had her whole marriage been a lie?

Wyatt drove for a while, gripping the steering wheel.

Please, God, help me to let go of this anger.

Christine had pushed a button when she had criticized the way he did his job. *She* had gone from being an investigator in a crime to being connected to it, however indirectly. Those questions had to be asked.

Of course she was upset. He knew she would be. He'd been careful in his word choice. He would never let his personal feelings interfere with his work. It bothered him that she thought he would.

As his truck rolled up and down the hills and he prayed, peace returned. At least he hadn't lost it in front of Christine. She didn't deserve his anger. She never had.

What bothered him more than anything, what ate at his gut, was that he couldn't go back in time and treat Christine like she deserved to be treated. Her lack of trust in him made her question his motives. He wanted her to see that he had changed, but all the wounds from the past interfered with that.

Wyatt neared a crossroads and turned on his blinker. The acid in his stomach chewed away at his insides. He had to let go of the idea that he could redeem himself in Christine's eyes, that he could win back her trust. He had done too much damage ten years ago.

Wyatt returned to the hotel and took a much-needed nap. When he woke up to the sound of his cell phone ringing, it was dark outside his window. He picked up the phone, hoping it was Christine calling to say she wanted to talk.

The number wasn't hers.

"Hello," he said.

"Agent Green? This is Deputy Mitchell. I've got some information for you that I thought might be helpful. I don't know if it's important or not. I've had my feelers out to people who I know aren't going to blab—you know, just asking them to notice anything unusual or if people they don't recognize come into their stores, especially someone with a kid."

With a sense of renewed hope, Wyatt sat up on the end of his bed. "Someone spotted Emmett and Tyler?"

Deputy Mitchell let out a little laugh. "Not quite that straightforward. My friend who works at The Trading Post in Placerville said two men she didn't recognize came in. They bought the usual supplies, but then they also wanted stuff for a little boy—T-shirts, toys, that sort of thing."

"Did either man match Emmett Lansky's description?"

"No, both these guys were big, overweight, potbellied. From the photograph you showed us, Lansky was in top-notch shape," Mitchell said.

So Lansky might be having someone run errands for him while he hid out, and it didn't sound as if they were locals. "Did these guys mention where they were going?"

"They didn't say, and my friend didn't think to notice which direction they headed when they left."

"Thanks, maybe we'll concentrate our search closer to Placerville." Not knowing which direction the men had gone meant they wouldn't be able to narrow things down much, but Placerville was the same place Christine had encountered Champlain acting suspicious. "I assume you have kept Chris . . . Sheriff Norris in the loop about this?"

"Well, that's just the thing. The reason why I called you is that I can't get ahold of her. I know it's late, but she's not answering her cell, which is practically attached to her body. I couldn't get her when I tried her landline, either."

"But I was just at her house a few hours ago." Wyatt felt the hairs prickle on the back of his neck as he stared at the dark sky outside. "This is uncharacteristic for her?"

"Yes. I'm on my way to a domestic-disturbance call or I would just drive out there."

Wyatt rose to his feet and grabbed his coat. "I'll go check on her."

Time seemed to slow down as his truck rolled up and down the hills of the winding dirt road. He tapped his thumb on the steering wheel, scrambling for an explanation that made sense. It could just be that Christine was in a deep sleep or had let the batteries on her cell phone run down. No, that didn't make sense. She was on call 24/7 as the sheriff. She wouldn't do that.

His headlights illuminated the stand of trees that was the last landmark before the ranch came into view. Even before he saw the outbuildings, he saw the smoke rising up in the air. The old farmhouse was on fire.

SEVEN

By the time Wyatt got to the ranch, he could see the flames shooting out from the kitchen. He braked and jumped out of his car, grabbing a flashlight from his glove compartment with one hand and dialing 911 with the other.

He circled the house until he heard a dog

barking. Jake stood beside Eva. Dressed only in a thin nightgown, she had crossed her arms to stave off the cold. Adrenaline surged through him when he saw no sign of Christine or Grandma Maggie.

Wyatt ran to Eva, shining the light toward her. Her eyes were wide with fear. Ignoring Jake's barking and protective stance, Wyatt touched Eva's upper arm. "Are you okay?" The rising panic made it hard for him to keep his voice even, but for Eva's sake he had to remain calm.

The little girl nodded. "Mommy told me to stay put."

"Where are your mother and your grandmother?"

"Mommy had to go back inside to find Grandma Maggie." Eva gripped Wyatt's forearm. "It's been a long time. Where is she?" The little girl was shivering.

"I'll go get them." He patted her arm. "You did good. Stay right here like your mom said." He slipped out of his jacket and placed it over her shoulders. "Keep warm."

Wyatt circled back to the front of the house. The front door was locked. It looked as if the actual fire was in the kitchen, not the living room or bedroom areas. The danger, then, was smoke inhalation. He found a cistern that captured rainwater from the roof, tore a piece of his shirt off and dampened it.

He didn't have time to figure out what window

Christine had crawled through to get back in if the front door was still locked. Placing the cloth over his mouth, he kicked down the front door and dived inside.

Thick smoke assaulted him. His eyes watered. In the darkness and the smoke, he could not see or hear anything.

Christine coughed and hefted Maggie's arm over her shoulder to carry her out. She'd found the older woman lying immobile in her bed, breathing, but unresponsive. Maggie's room was the closest to the kitchen and she always took a sleeping pill before bed. The older woman had breathed in enough smoke to pass out.

Christine sank under the weight of Maggie's uncooperative body. Maggie was not a big woman, but because she was unconscious, she was deadweight. Christine coughed again. How long did she have before she passed out? Crawling out on the floor where there was less smoke was out of the question. She wouldn't be able to drag Maggie out that way.

Stepping forward, bracing her arm around Maggie's waist, she reached out for what she thought was the open window in Eva's room, the one she had broken and crawled out of with her daughter. Instead she touched the coatrack in the hallway. She'd gotten turned around in the house and become completely disoriented. Strength left her body. Her throat was gritty from inhaling smoke, and she felt light-headed.

Christine said a quick prayer. She wasn't about to let either of them die. She loved Maggie like a mother.

Each breath took substantial effort as her brain fogged. She stepped in what she hoped was the right direction. "Come on . . . Maggie. I'm not going to leave you here."

Her grip on Maggie loosened. Despite her resolve, her arms and legs didn't cooperate. She sank down to the floor.

Please, God, no. Who will take care of Eva?

A voice, strong and clear, broke through the smoke. "Christine."

"Here. We're here." Her words sounded as if they died before they even got out of her throat. "Over here." She swooned and struggled to stay alert.

A strong arm grasped her hand and then wrapped around her waist. She heard the voice in her ear say, "I've got you. You're all right now."

"Maggie?"

"I've got her, too. I can't carry you both. You are going to have to follow me out. Hold on here." He placed a piece of fabric in her hand, his shirt-tail.

Christine could not see anything. She had no idea what room they were in. She felt the floor beneath her bare feet and the fabric in her hand as he led her out. With only darkness and smoke around her, she had to trust him.

As though she had broken through the water's surface, she saw blurry lights and wheezed in fresh air. She continued to cough. Strong arms encircled her, holding her, brushing the hair out of her eyes. Her hand rested against the hard muscles of Wyatt's chest.

His voice was gentle as he held her. "You okay?"

She managed a nod.

Then she felt Eva's small hand in her own. Jake's soft fur brushed against her arms.

Praise God.

The sense of relief almost made her laugh, but her laugh turned into a cough. The warm arms that held her vaporized. Slowly, her vision cleared. In the distance, she could see the flashing lights of the volunteer firefighters coming up the road.

Flames shot out from the kitchen roof, which grew blacker by the moment.

Eva crawled into Christine's lap. She held her daughter. Her heart raced, she smelled of smoke and her lungs felt seared, but she was alive. She closed her eyes, clung to her precious daughter and cried. When she opened her eyes, she turned slightly on the bench where Wyatt had gently placed her.

A few feet away, Wyatt had laid Grandma Maggie on the ground. He'd gotten a blanket from somewhere, which he placed over her. Tenderly, he lifted her and placed something under her head for a pillow.

After he had helped Maggie, he picked a bottle off the ground and walked over to Christine. There was a splotch of black across his forehead. His shirt was unbuttoned and torn.

He handed her the water bottle. "From my truck."

She took the water bottle, offering Eva a sip first. Maggie still didn't move beneath the blanket. Christine tilted her head. "Is she—"

"She's starting to come to. She murmured when I said her name."

The siren from the fire truck broke through the night air.

Christine looked up at Wyatt. "Thank you."

"I'm glad you're all right." Self-conscious, he turned to the side and buttoned up his shirt.

The fire truck pulled into the yard and five men jumped out. One of them ran over to Christine and Wyatt.

"Do you have a water source we can tap into?"

"There's a spigot over by the barn and a rainwater cistern closer to the house by the garden." Christine tried to clear the grittiness out of her throat by swallowing more water.

Wyatt slapped a flat hand on the man's back. "Thank you for coming. We've got an older woman over here who needs medical attention."

"I'll send the doc over." The young fireman

looked at Christine and then Eva. "He'll take a look at all of you."

"I can give you a hand with getting this fire put out," Wyatt said. He turned back to look at Christine. "If you're okay with me leaving you here?"

She nodded. Wyatt ran over to the truck and waited for instructions from a paunchy man who Christine recognized as her downriver neighbor. An older man made his way toward Christine.

"Hey, Doctor Romney." Her voice was hoarse.

He offered her a smile and comforting squeeze of her shoulder. "Looks like you have had a busy night."

"Could you look at Maggie first? She's in worse shape than me." The doctor nodded and strode over to where Maggie still lay on the grass.

Wyatt ran back over to Christine and handed her a man's fleece sweatshirt. "It was in the fire truck. Thought you might be getting cold." She took the shirt. Shock from the trauma had masked her shivering, but her thin nightgown was no good against the evening chill.

Wyatt ran back toward the fire, picked up a bucket and disappeared around the side of the house.

"He must be cold," Eva said. "He gave me his coat."

Christine slipped into the sweatshirt, appreciating how it warmed her. "That was very thoughtful of him, wasn't it?" She gathered her daughter back into her arms, tucking Wyatt's coat around her legs. She cupped her hands over Eva's bare feet.

Her throat felt as if it had been scraped with a utility knife and her muscles were like cooked noodles. Pain shot through her injured shoulder. She had cuts on her hand from where she had broken the window with one of Eva's dolls.

But I'm alive. Thanks to Wyatt, we're all alive.

She brushed her fingers through Eva's brown curls and said a silent prayer of thanks. The doctor had gotten Maggie to sit up. He wrapped the blanket around her shoulders as she looked around.

Christine called to her. "Maggie, come over and sit with us on the bench."

The doctor held out a hand and helped Maggie to her feet. With the doctor's support, she shuffled toward the bench and eased herself down beside Christine. Christine patted the older woman's leg, and both their eyes filled with tears.

"You three should have some oxygen. I want to see all of you in my office first thing for chest X-rays so we can check the extent of the smoke damage." He turned back toward the house where the flames had lessened. "What do you suppose caused the fire?"

Christine stared at the part of the house that used to be her kitchen. The roof was half-gone, exposing the interior of the room. Bits of black debris fell to the ground. "I don't know. It started in the kitchen. Maybe something got left on."

Maggie shook her head. "No, I always turn everything off."

Grandma Maggie had never been forgetful before. "I made a cup of tea before I went to bed." She gave Maggie's hand a reassuring pat. "I might have forgotten something." But even that didn't make sense. From the look of the damage, the fire must have spread so quickly that by the time the smoke woke her up, the fire was out of control.

The doctor put his hands on his hips. "Lot of these older places have compromised wiring. Hard to say what it was." He stepped away from them. "I've got a kit in the fire truck to treat those cuts."

The doctor returned a moment later. He disinfected and bandaged Christine's cuts and treated her leg for first-degree burn. Though she couldn't remember when, she must at some point gotten close to the fire. Except for the smoke inhalation and the emotional trauma, Eva and Maggie checked out okay.

Wyatt continued to help the men until the flames died down and only the blackened shell of the kitchen remained. His chest and face had gotten grimy from the effort, but his energy never waned.

Maggie rested her head on Christine's shoulder, and the three women huddled together. "Looks like they got it before it spread."

"The smoke damage is through the whole house. We'll have to find a place in town to stay. I'll talk to Lonnie DePaul at the insurance office in the morning. Maybe our policy covers rent." Now that she had calmed down from all the excitement, fatigue had set in. Eva already slumbered in her arms.

"I'm sure Arlene from church can put us up for the night," said Grandma Maggie.

Christine leaned against Maggie. "Once we find out what the insurance will cover, we can rebuild." Her heart ached at the loss of the farmhouse that had been home for over ten years.

Wyatt walked over to them. He swiped at his forehead with the back of his hand. "They've about got things wrapped up out here. Do you have a place to stay in town?"

Christine nodded. Eva stirred and opened her eyes. "What about my shiny black shoes." The little girl clung to the stuffed animal she always slept with, which smelled like smoke. "I don't think they are going to let us go back inside to get your shoes just yet. You know what that means, don't you?"

"What?" Eva said weakly.

"We get to buy brand-new shoes and a brand-new dress." For her daughter's sake, Christine tried to inject enthusiasm in her voice, but it fell flat.

Eva gripped Christine's collar and pressed close to her. "I liked my old shoes."

At the very least, the house would have to be gutted and most of their possessions thrown away because of the smoke damage. Christine closed her eyes. She didn't want to think about that now. They were alive. That was all that mattered.

She tugged on Wyatt's coat to free it from Eva. "You're probably getting cold."

"I want to keep it," Eva whispered with her face against Christine's chest. The little girl pulled the coat out of Christine's fingers and wrapped it around herself again. Christine doubted she could pry the stinky stuffed animal from Eva, either. These were all the little girl's worldly possessions, all she had left, and she wasn't going to part with them easily.

"She can keep it," said Wyatt. "If you want, I can take you into town."

Christine rose to her feet and sat Eva on the ground. His kindness moved her deeply, and she had no strength to drive herself. She reached out and rubbed a dark streak off his cheek. "You saved our lives."

Wyatt brushed the comment away. "I just did what needed to be done." His voice was thick with emotion. The power of his gaze held her in place. There was something more he wasn't saying. There was always something more he wasn't saying.

The volunteer firefighters had begun to pack up their gear and hoses. One by one, all of them came over and offered condolences and made sure she had a place to stay. Some of them she didn't know by name, but all of the men she recognized as her neighbors.

Maggie ran to her own car where she retrieved her purse and cell phone. Christine's cell phone and purse were somewhere in the house. Christine held a hand out for Maggie and the three of them trudged to Wyatt's truck. Once Wyatt got behind the wheel, Christine slipped in beside him. Eva sat between Christine and Maggie. Jake, the border collie, rode in the back of the truck.

Within minutes, both Maggie and Eva fell asleep. There was something comforting about being next to Wyatt. She leaned against him, relishing the sense of safety she had when she was close to him. "How did you know to come back out to the ranch?"

He filled her in on the call from Deputy Mitchell.

Christine shook her head. "The little town of Placerville does seem to be important in all this. There are three main roads that lead out from there and countless others that intersect and branch off." The adrenaline from getting out of the fire was wearing off as a mixture of shock and weariness spread through her. "It's hard to think about anything but that fire right now."

Wyatt asked, "I assume you had insurance?" The lights of town came into view.

Christine nodded.

"There'll be an investigation, then?"

"I'm sure there will at least be an assessment of the damage before they do a payout," she said. "We certainly didn't start the fire on purpose." Her suspicions aroused, she asked, "What are you thinking?"

"Nothing. Let's just focus on you guys getting to a safe place and getting some sleep."

She appreciated that he didn't want to make her anxious over his speculations, but his question caused a memory to flash in her brain. Wyatt had looked into the exposed kitchen once the fire had died down. What had he seen? Did he think someone else had started the fire?

Christine's blood ran cold as her conversation with her hired hand, Larry Myers, in the equipment barn came to mind. She needed to find out what Larry had done after he left her place and where he had been when the fire started.

The whispered threat she had heard in her hospital room that night now seemed more real than imagined.

EIGHT

A wave of fatigue hit Christine as they drew near Arlene's house. She was tired. She was devastated. She needed a shower, but all she could think about was falling into a soft bed and wrapping the covers around her. Arlene was standing on the porch when they pulled up. Maggie had phoned her friend only moments before. Though she was wearing a housecoat and curlers, nothing in her demeanor suggested she had just been rousted out of bed. She offered an energetic wave as they pushed open truck doors and trudged up the stairs.

Arlene was a short, bent-over woman with a blue tinge to her white hair and a warm smile. "Come in, all of you, before you catch cold." She looked at Wyatt. "You, too. I'm sure you could use a hot cup of cocoa before you are on your way."

In the living room, Arlene had already piled a stack of folded blankets on the couch. She touched Eva's cheek. "Poor dears, you've been through so much." She bustled into the kitchen. "Now, sit down, all of you. The water is already hot."

Christine had the feeling that Arlene was the kind of person you didn't argue with. The four of them had barely spoken a word to each other since driving away from the burned house. The trauma had caused them all to fall into a numb silence. Eva crawled into her lap. Christine closed her eyes and rested her cheek against the top of Eva's head.

They sat in silence while Arlene bustled in the kitchen. She returned a few minutes later with a tray full of steaming mugs. "I've got a guest bedroom and a fold-out couch." She handed a mug to each one of them. "If anyone needs to shower, that is open to you, too."

Maggie tucked a wayward strand of hair behind her ear. "Thank you, Arlene . . . for everything." Her eyes had lost their luster, and her shoulders drooped.

Arlene's voice flooded with compassion. "It's the least I can do, considering what you have been through. Go on, drink up your cocoa. I'll go see what I can rustle up in the way of pajamas and extra clothes and then we'll get you off to bed."

Eva slipped off Christine's lap and walked over to a chair where a poodle slept. She stroked the little dog and pressed her face close to it. Jake had settled in a corner after sniffing most of the items in the living room.

The chocolate and warmth soothed Christine as she sipped the cocoa.

Wyatt's cell phone vibrated. He flipped it open. "A text message from Cranson. Looks like he sent one earlier, too."

"What does it say?"

"Both the messages say to come to the Cattleman's Café," Wyatt said. "He doesn't say what he wants to talk about. I'm sure it has something to do with the case. He wouldn't have texted this late if it wasn't important."

"I'll go with you." Even as she started to get out of the chair, fatigue weighed her down. Wyatt must be just as exhausted.

He placed a hand on her shoulder. "You stay here and get some sleep. I can brief you in the morning. Just give me directions to the café."

Christine glanced at Eva, who had climbed into the chair, gathered the poodle in her arms and fallen asleep. Maggie, as well, had started to nod off. She was having a hard time keeping her eyes open. She wouldn't be of much help to him, anyway.

"You must be tired, too," she said.

"I'll be all right," he reassured her.

She didn't have the energy to argue, but she still had professional duties. "Okay, let me know what you find out right away. Don't wait until morning." After giving him Arlene's phone number, she walked with him to the door and watched through the window as he got into his truck. The harsh glare of his red taillight faded in the distance. She returned to the couch and collapsed.

The Cattleman's Café was a small freestanding building with barn wood siding and gingham curtains in the window. A single light glowed inside the café, but the sign on the window said the café closed at ten o'clock. Wyatt checked his watch—it was nearly ten-thirty. The only car in the parking lot was his.

Wyatt got out of the truck and looked around. Across the road was a much larger building with a sign out front that said Roosevelt Stockyards. The first text had come in around nine-thirty while he was still out dealing with the fire. Maybe Cranson hadn't realized the place closed down at ten. Wyatt walked around the dark café and then he noticed Cranson's truck parked on the side of the stockyards in the shadows. As he drew nearer to the stockyards, the lowing of cattle and the smell of manure and hay became more prominent. Cranson's truck was unlocked, and it was the only truck in the lot. Had Cranson found something in the stockyards that was connected to the case? Or had he just decided to park in this lot after the café closed?

The back end of the stockyards consisted of a series of corrals and chutes that allowed workers to funnel and sort the cows. From having been in other stockyards, he suspected that the inside was a pavilion with bleacher-style seating where prospective buyers could view and bid on cattle when they were brought in.

As he circled around to where the cattle were, a back door to the pavilion banged in the wind. Odd that with millions of dollars worth of cattle lined up for sale, there wasn't more security. It seemed a dangerous oversight to have left a door open. Wyatt climbed over a metal fence into a corral that contained about twenty cows, who weren't at all alarmed by his presence. They watched him with their liquid onyx eyes. The bull one corral over, though, stomped his feet and snorted. Wyatt was grateful for the fence between them.

He wove through the corrals to the open door, careful to avoid any bull that would regard him as a trespasser. He had intended to latch the door, but a flash of light drew his attention. He stepped through the door and found himself inside the building in a corral with a concrete floor with a thin layer of hay on it. Stretching out in front of him was bleacher-style seating for prospective buyers. To his right was a small door marked Office. From where he stood, he had the cow's-eye view to his surroundings. So this was what it felt like to be sold at auction.

He stepped closer to the bleachers and studied his surroundings. Above him was a crow's nest that had been visible from the outside, as well. Whoever sat up there had a view of the cows in the corral and the action inside. Across from him was a second viewing pen with a door to the outside.

The mooing of the cattle had grown louder outside as though something was stirring them up.

With only the light spilling through a window from a lamppost, he couldn't see the second corral clearly, but it looked as if there was a lump on the ground.

Wyatt took out his key ring with a flashlight on it and shone it toward the second pen. His breath hitched. The lump was Cranson lying facedown in the dirt. Outside, the clamor from the cows had grown even louder. As he ran toward his friend, he heard metal scrape against metal. Someone was moving the cows around outside.

When he touched his partner's shoulder, he was unresponsive. The screeching of metal and the stomping of hooves grew louder, more intense. Wyatt flipped Cranson over. Blood oozed from the top of his head, but he had a pulse.

Anchoring his elbows under Cranson's armpits, he attempted to drag him toward the edge of the pen. The man was heavier than he looked.

The outside door burst open, and a bull lumbered into the pen. He swayed back and forth and lowered his head.

Heart hammering in his chest, Wyatt slung the unconscious Cranson on the metal fence hoping to heft him over the top. The bull grunted and then thousands of pounds of pure muscle charged toward them.

Startled awake, Christine rose from the couch where she had dozed off. The house was quiet and dark. Arlene must have ushered Eva and Maggie off to bed and then gone to sleep herself.

Disturbing images and sounds from the fire had awakened her as she relived them in her dreams. She couldn't have been asleep more than twenty minutes. The nightmare had left her feeling unsettled. Despite weariness, she wasn't sure if she could go back to sleep. She didn't want to close her eyes only to hear Eva's screams again.

Christine paced for a few minutes, hoping that would work off the nerves and calm her down enough to go back to sleep. No luck. She clicked on a lamp. Taking action would help her deal with the anxious thoughts.

She picked up Arlene's phone. Despite the late hour, it had taken only a few phone calls to find out that Larry Myers had been drinking at a bar for most of the time after he had made his veiled threat and left Christine's property. Still, there were ways to start fires so that the burn would be delayed and the arsonist would be miles from the scene of the crime. Wyatt certainly was suspicious.

She looked around at the homey but unfamiliar kitchen. A dagger stabbed at her heart, taking her breath away. Her house was gone. The home she and Dustin had lived in together. Even though most of the house was only smoke damaged, she was pretty sure there would be very little she could salvage.

She wandered into the kitchen and pulled a tea bag out of the little canister Arlene kept on the counter. The devastation of the fire signaled an end to a season of her life. The season she had spent with Dustin as his wife.

Maybe it was a blessing in disguise. She had hung on to the ranch because it was what Dustin had loved. In a way, staying there had allowed her to not fully let go of Dustin.

She flipped the burner on and placed the teakettle on it. Now a cloud hung over Dustin's life because of his connection to Harrison Van Norman. She'd been hasty in accusing Wyatt of letting his hurt from the past cast a shadow on Dustin. Maybe those questions did need to be asked. She didn't want the past ten years of her life to be a lie. If there was only a way to find out why Dustin stayed friends with Harrison.

Christine glanced up at the kitchen clock. It was nearly eleven. She had asked Wyatt to call no matter what he found out. The phone was only a few feet from the couch. She would have heard it ring even in a deep sleep.

Her heart skipped a beat when she looked at the clock again. The Cattleman's Café closed at ten o'clock. Why would Cranson want to meet Wyatt at a café that was already locked up? Maybe the first text message had been sent when the café was open, but the second message should have rerouted Wyatt to a place that was open.

Quelling any rising panic, she picked up Arlene's phone and dialed Wyatt's cell number. It rang five times before going to message. He wasn't the type to turn his phone off just so he could get some sleep. His sense of duty to the job ran deeper than that.

Christine turned the burner off and raced into the living room. She grabbed the pants and shirt Arlene had dug up for her to wear in the morning off the back of the couch. She ran to the powder room. By the time she had changed out of her smoke-damaged nightgown, her heart was beating a mile a minute. A sense of urgency threatened to overwhelm her.

She grabbed the keys to Arlene's car, which Arlene had given her permission to borrow in the morning. She ran out to the car and drove through the empty streets of downtown Roosevelt, though it hurt her shoulder.

Her gun was back at the house, and the other guns were locked away at the sheriff's office. Instinct told her that there wasn't enough time to retrieve it. The stockyards with the café beside it appeared in silhouette as she rounded the curve. A single lamppost and a half-moon provided the only light. As she drew near, she saw Wyatt's truck by the café with the single light on inside. She pulled into the lot beside his truck and got out.

Cranson's truck was parked closer to the stockyards. Something was making the cattle restless.

She jogged over to the entrance of the stockyards. The structure didn't have any windows and the door was locked.

An odd piercing sound came from inside. Her heart thudded in her chest. Shots were being fired inside the pavilion. There had to be another way in.

Her feet pounded through the gravel lot as she ran around to the back where the cattle were. Her eyes traveled up to the crow's nest where she had seen a flash of movement. Someone was up there with a rifle. Christine scooted easily through the corral filled with heifers and calves.

She lifted the latch that secured the back door where the cattle were herded into viewing pens. A second shot made her heart seize up. She'd come in on the side closest to the crow's nest. Noise drew her attention across the pavilion. She could just make out Wyatt attempting to drag a limp body up the bleachers. A third shot splintered the wood on the bench, inches from where Wyatt was. Lack of light was the only thing working against the shooter.

Christine pressed against the wall, out of view of the shooter in the crow's nest. Going directly toward the bleachers would just make her another target.

She scrambled into the second viewing pen that contained a large bull. Moving quickly through the pen allowed the bull only a moment to register that she was close, not enough time to show aggression. She made soothing sounds as she drew near the huge bull. Using the bull as a site shield, she was able to get closer to Wyatt before the shooter had even noticed her. Now she could see that Wyatt was trying to drag Cranson's body up the bleachers.

She leaped up the bleachers toward him. When she drew close enough, Wyatt's face registered recognition as he anchored his arms under Cranson's armpits.

Cranson's head tilted to one side. Wyatt lifted his elbow. "Pistol's in the holster. I can't reach it without letting go of him."

Christine reached around Cranson's back and pulled the gun free of the holster. A handgun wouldn't give her enough accuracy to hit the crow's nest, but maybe she could scare the shooter away or create a diversion so Wyatt could get Cranson to safety. She ran toward the crow's nest where the figure stood in shadow. Not as clear as he had been outside with the lamppost shining on him.

The glass window of the crow's nest slid shut. She heard footsteps. The man must have seen her and was trying to escape. She raced toward the back door. As she ran through it, she could hear the sound of feet going down stairs. She climbed three sets of fences to get to the side of the building where the stairs came out.

Rapid footsteps crunched over gravel, but she couldn't discern where the shooter was.

"Hold it. Police."

A rifle shot hit the side of the building inches from her head. Stunned, she shook her head and planted her feet, staring out into the darkness. Estimating where the shot had come from, she took aim and fired. The cordite smell from the pistol filled the night air as silence descended around her.

She doubted she had hit her target. There was no cry of pain. She hadn't heard footsteps, either. Christine took in a breath. Her heartbeat drummed in her ears. She could detect no movement, no sound. Where was he? Seconds passed. She waited for her eyes to adjust to the darkness, hoping to see something.

Footsteps pounded toward her. She had time to do a half turn before a hard body slammed into her, lifted her up and banged her against the wall of the pavilion. With the wind knocked out of her, it took a moment for Christine to comprehend what had happened and another moment to feel around on the ground for the gun and struggle to her feet. She coughed from the blow to her stomach and pain radiated through her injured shoulder.

The man was escaping back toward the corrals. Still recovering from the pummeling she'd taken, she ran as fast as she could. There was enough light to see the man as he wove his way through the livestock. He'd disappear and then his head would appear again in a different corral like a man diving under water, swimming a ways and rising to the surface.

Wyatt came through the same door she had used.

"He went that way." Christine pointed and yelled across the expanse of corrals.

"I'll circle around," Wyatt shouted over his shoulder as he jumped the fence and searched around the other side of the corrals.

Moving in the opposite direction of Wyatt, Christine worked her way around the perimeter of the corrals, scanning the interior for any sign of movement that might be human. The cows had calmed down from their earlier rousting and gave away no indication they might be housing a fugitive.

She and Wyatt met at the far end of the corrals, which were shrouded in darkness.

Wyatt shone his flashlight on the corrals closest to them. "I don't see him."

She tried to shake off the creeping sense of disappointment as she turned and stared into the surrounding blackness. "He could have slipped out underneath a fence somewhere."

"I didn't hear a car start. He must still be on foot," Wyatt said.

"Still . . . I think it would be an act of futility to try to chase him."

His hand slipped into hers, and he squeezed it tight. "I think you saved my life back there."

As the warmth of his touch permeated her skin, she relaxed, letting go of the frustration of not being able to catch the shooter. "That makes us even for today. You pulled me from a burning house."

"How did you know I was in trouble?" He leaned a little closer to her. His shoulder touched hers.

"Too many things felt off. You didn't call. And I couldn't figure out why Cranson was having you come to a café that was closed." She turned to face him. "How is Cranson, anyway? He looked like he was hurt."

Wyatt rested a hand on the corral. "He's okay. He was starting to come to after I left him. He took a bad blow to the head and his ankle may be broken."

"What happened?"

"Someone left a message at the motel desk that they knew something about the bombing and that they would meet at the café. Cranson said the first text message was his, but the second one must have been sent by whoever knocked him out and grabbed his phone. I think someone was trying to put us both out of commission by luring me here. Two federal agents for the price of one. Any theories on who might want to do that?"

Christine's stomach wrenched. "Nobody in

town is comfortable with the feds being here." She lifted her head toward the crow's nest in the distance. "This was pretty violent, though . . . I just can't imagine any of the townspeople going this far because of what happened ten years ago."

They walked back toward Cranson's truck. "It must be connected to us looking into the bombing. The evidence response team was here less than five hours. We really have tried not to raise suspicions or be disruptive."

When they arrived at Cranson's truck, the door was open and Cranson was conscious but slumped forward. He raised his head. "Hey, you two, are we having a fun night here or what?" His tone was joking, but the tension line between his eyebrows and gritted teeth gave away how much pain he was in.

Wyatt's voice filled with compassion for his friend and partner. "I don't think you are fit to drive. Let me take you over to the hospital. I'll retrieve your car tomorrow."

The older man didn't argue as Wyatt held out an arm to help Cranson walk while he favored his left leg. After locking up Cranson's car, they walked back to the café parking lot. Wyatt helped Cranson into the passenger side of his truck and walked over to where Christine stood by her borrowed car, resting her hand on the top of the door.

"That guy might still be out here somewhere.

I'll follow you into town just to make sure you're safely back inside at Arlene's place." His hand covered hers.

"Thank you," she said.

"Quite a night, huh?" Without giving her time to answer, he leaned toward her and covered her lips with his. He pulled away as quickly as he had kissed her. "You saved my life."

The kiss brought back a flood of memories. Some things about Wyatt had always been wonderful. She was still reeling from the kiss when she bent down to get into the car.

She started the car, switched on the headlights and pulled out onto the road. When she looked in her rearview mirror the warm glow of Wyatt's headlights was a comfort.

True to his word, he followed her all the way into town and waited on the street until she was safely inside. As she watched him turn around and pull out, she wondered what he had meant by his quick kiss.

NINE

Christine shoved her hands in the pockets of her coat as she stood outside Roosevelt's only insurance office. The events of the previous night weighed heavily on her.

A bitter chill had replaced the balmy spring weather. It had begun to feel like Mohler County was headed back into winter instead of toward spring. She buttoned the top button against the cold and made her way toward the glass door that read Lonnie DePaul Life Auto Home. Apprehension twisted the muscles at the back of her neck into a knot. She didn't want to think about the fire, but this had to be done.

Christine took a deep breath and pushed open the door. Lonnie DePaul had been the only insurance salesman in town for over twenty years. He was a large, red-cheeked man known for being the biggest supporter and loudest fan at high-school basketball games.

Lonnie offered her a broad grin. "Christine, how good to see you." He rose from his chair and placed a beefy hand over hers. "So sorry to hear about the farmhouse."

"I'm sure you were expecting me."

"I've already got a call into one of our insurance adjusters. He's driving over and I'm meeting him out at your place this afternoon."

"We're going to have to rent a place in town while it's rebuilt. Is there any sort of coverage for that?"

"As you know, I can't give you any firm numbers on final settlement until after the adjuster gives me numbers and the fire marshal determines the cause of the fire." Lonnie sat back in his chair, which emitted a creak from his weight. He laced his fingers behind his head. Sweat stains showed on the armpits of his button-down shirt.

"Lonnie, you know Maggie and me. You know we wouldn't start that fire on purpose."

"Of course I do. We got to jump through the insurance-company hoops. You know that." He lumbered over to the file cabinet and pulled open a drawer. "I have this all on computer, but I still like looking at the hard copy."

Lonnie sat down in his chair. He leaned forward and flipped open the folder, studying it for a moment. He perused another page. "It looks like you have loss-of-use coverage for alternative housing. After you meet your deductible, I can give you a small emergency payment and then you just keep track of receipts for housing, food, laundry, and we will reimburse you."

Christine collapsed into a chair. "That's good news." She swiped at the tears that formed in her eyes. "I didn't mean to start crying like this."

"You've been through a lot. These kind of things hit you like a brick wall. You think you are doing okay and then whammo. I've seen it a thousand times with my clients. Even something as small as a fender bender. It shakes you up."

Christine didn't dare say anything for fear she might start crying again. Instead, she laced her hands together and stared at the ceiling.

Lonnie rose to his feet and let out a huff of air.

"How is Eva doing? Is she about ready for junior varsity?"

She appreciated his efforts at lightening the mood. "She's only five, Lonnie."

"You know my recruiting efforts for the Fighting Eagles starts early. Wait here just a minute. I think I have something she might like." Lonnie disappeared into a back room.

Christine could hear him moving boxes and shuffling around. She stared at the open file of the insurance policy on the desk and then leaned forward. Lonnie had grabbed two file folders by accident. The second folder was also marked Norris.

Christine's throat went dry. The second folder must have been the life-insurance payout on Dustin. She pulled the folder across the desk and flipped it open. Wyatt's questions about Dustin's association with Harrison still haunted her. She knew the answers wouldn't be in a dry insurance report, but she felt the need to fill in the memories that her grief had blotted out after the accident. The top page was a typed report of the accident. She skimmed.

It had been raining the day Dustin died. The ground was muddy. The report suggested he may have slipped when his hand was stuck in the baler as he was repairing it. Underneath the report was a photograph of the bloodstained hay baler. She studied the photo for a moment then closed the folder when the familiar heartache returned. She shoved the report back on the desk. Some memories didn't need to be resurrected.

Lonnie emerged from the back room, holding a folded purple-and-yellow shirt, the Eagles colors. "This should fit her."

Lonnie must keep boxes of assorted sizes of Eagles shirts. "Thanks, Lonnie. It's never too early to create a fan." She rose to her feet.

Lonnie patted Christine's back. "We should be able to get that check to you for rental expenses fairly quickly." He leaned a little closer to her. "You look tired."

"It's not just the fire. I've been working with the FBI to connect the dots on this bombing."

Lonnie took a step back. A shadow descended over his features. "Yes, of course, the FBI," he seethed.

Lonnie was the last person she had expected to see such a disdainful response from. Taken aback, and not sure how to respond to his sudden change in mood, she thanked him and stepped back out into the overcast day. Though she had only looked at it for a moment, the photograph of the hay baler was seared into her mind. When she closed her eyes, she saw the blood and the muddy ground around it and what vaguely looked like two sets of footprints. She recognized the tread of Dustin's work boots. The other pair had had a distinctive waffle print.

Christine shoved her hands in her pockets and headed up the street. It could be that the second set of footprints was the insurance investigator's, but it seemed as if they would be careful about that sort of thing.

Across the street, Wyatt's truck tore into the sheriff's office parking lot and came to a screeching halt. Wyatt jumped out and raced into the sheriff's office.

Sensing some urgency, Christine crossed the street at a run and went directly into the office. Wyatt whirled around to face her.

Her first thought was that something more had happened to Wyatt's partner. "Is Cranson okay?"

"He's going to be laid up for a while, but that is not why I came here. Have you gotten a cell phone yet?"

"No, I haven't had time to get a new one, and I don't know if the old one is still in service back at the house."

"I've been looking for you. I went by Arlene's. I just heard from your deputy. She did a drive by Champlain's house on her way to another call. He's packing up."

"Let's take your truck. It's more generic than the sheriff's vehicle." She pulled a pair of binoculars off a hook. "If we have to tail him close I don't want to give ourselves away." Christine grabbed her gun belt from a drawer. "We'd better get out there before he leaves."

• • •

Adrenaline moved through Wyatt's veins like quicksilver as they neared Champlain's house. Tailing him had to open up the investigation. Champlain was at best a tenuous link to Emmett Lansky's location. The connections between all the men involved laid out like a web. Champlain tied to Randy Stiller, Randy had robbed the bank with Harrison Van Norman and Harrison was a known associate of Lansky's. How Dustin Norris fit into that picture he wasn't sure.

"There, that stand of trees will shield us." Christine pointed.

Wyatt steered the truck off the road toward the trees as quickly as he could. They slipped out of the truck without a word, being careful to shut the doors softly. Christine put the binoculars around her neck and settled behind a large rock that served to shield her from view. A truck containing a motorcycle designed for off-road use in the truck bed stood in Champlain's driveway. Wyatt crouched beside Christine and peered over the rock. No sign of any activity.

"This brings back some memories," he whispered, leaning closer to her. The sensation of last night's kiss still seared his senses. He had been impulsive, but almost losing her in the fire and then his own life at the stockyards made him realize that time was short. He didn't want to live his life wondering if they could make it work. He needed to know. He needed to act on his feelings even if it meant getting hurt.

Christine turned toward him. "What do you mean?"

Her voice warmed him to the marrow. "You and me doing surveillance together."

Christine nodded as she brought the binoculars up to her eyes. A faint smile crossed her lips as though a good memory had flitted through her head. "Like old times."

Was she thinking about the kiss, too?

The spot they had chosen was uphill from Champlain's small house by about a hundred yards. A wooden fence in need of painting surrounded the house. Two other houses of similar design stood on either side of Champlain's. Each lot looked to be about an acre. The front door opened and a black Lab gamboled out sniffing the brown grass.

Champlain emerged from the house carrying a pack for the motorcycle, which he threw in the truck bed. After petting the dog, he disappeared inside the garage and returned a few minutes later with a gas can.

"Looks like we got here just in time," Wyatt whispered.

"I told Deputy Mitchell to wait at the crossroads once she got done with her call. She'll be able to tell us which way he turned. I'm pretty familiar with the roads around here. When we know which direction he is headed, there are roads that loop around each other so we can keep track of him without being behind him the whole time and risking him figuring out he's being tailed."

Champlain came out of his house again carrying two gun cases. He placed the cases on the front seat and whistled for his dog. Once the Lab was settled on the passenger side, Champlain got in and backed out of the driveway.

Christine spoke into the two-way radio. "He's on the move."

Through the static, she could hear Deputy Mitchell's voice. "Roger that. I'll let you know when I see him."

Christine leaned close to Wyatt and whispered, "Let's load up."

Wyatt got into the driver's side of the truck. "How long do you think it will be?"

She checked her watch. "Takes about five minutes to get to that crossroads." Christine's gaze flitted over to Wyatt several times. The look of affection in her eyes made his skin tingle.

The radio glitched and Christine pressed the button. "Go ahead, Mitchell."

"He's headed east toward the Thomas homestead."

"Really?" Christine tilted her head. "Thanks, Mitchell. Over and out."

Wyatt had already started the engine. "You seemed surprised by where he turned."

"That's not the road you take to get to Placerville."

They were operating on the assumption that the camp was on one of the roads that led out of Placerville. "Wonder what that means."

"I'm not sure." As they approached the crossroads, Christine pointed through the windshield. "Go straight up that way toward where those grain silos are."

Wyatt thought he was pretty good at reading maps or layouts for buildings and keeping them in his head, but Christine's *look for the barn that is falling down and wait until after the water hole with a single cottonwood* instructions were cryptic. The landmarks she referenced on the flat stretch of prairie were easy to miss. "How do you do that, remember all these details?"

"You're just used to urban landscapes. Navigation is a little different when roads don't have names and sometimes the roads don't even look like roads." She bent forward in her seat and looked up at the sky. "Got a prairie storm moving in over there. Hopefully, it will break up before it gets to where we are."

Wyatt peered through the windshield. Off in the distance, there was no separation between the massive dark clouds and the sheet of black rain that reached to the ground. "That looks nasty."

"There's no mountains to break up the storm.

131

They gather power every mile of prairie they eat up."

Up ahead on the road, Champlain's truck appeared at the top of a hill and then disappeared down the other side.

"We're far enough back," Christine said. "He's not going to know we're following him. The landscape is open enough so we'll see him from time to time."

As they drove, the rain pattered on the metal roof of the truck. Wyatt checked the rearview mirror. No one was behind them.

Christine sat up a little straighter. "Look, he's turning."

Champlain's truck bounced down a road that must have become washboard from rain and dry spells. "Now what? He's going to know we're following him if we turn off, too."

"He's headed toward the base of that big butte." Christine closed her eyes. "Let me try to remember if there's another road that leads into there. Just keep going straight for now. We can always turn around."

"Maybe he's not up to anything. He might just be planning a dirt-bike ride." Wyatt pointed at the barren landscape opposite of where Champlain had turned. "What's off in that direction, anyway?"

The rain fell faster and lightning cracked the sky. "A few farms."

The view out the window had grown dark and grim. The storm was racing across the landscape, forming a cell that looked a little like a mushroom cloud reaching to the ground.

With a sudden and intense voracity, the rain fell. Wyatt slowed the truck as the gumbo road became muddy. The truck slid sideways. He muscled the truck back onto the road, leaning forward in his seat to stare through the windshield where visibility had been cut in half. "That storm sure moved in fast."

Christine gripped the dashboard as the truck sloshed from side to side. "You want me to take over driving? I'm used to these kinds of conditions."

His knuckles turned white as he gripped the steering wheel. Pain shot through his injured arm. "Not with your bad shoulder."

The truck swerved. Wyatt felt the back end slip out, falling off the edge of the road down the bank. He cranked the steering wheel and pressed the accelerator. The tires spun but didn't gain any traction. Christine gripped the door handle as they careened off the high embankment of the road. They sat with the nose of the truck facing upward.

Wyatt pressed the accelerator. The wheels spun in the wet clay. "I was pretty sure that was a futile idea, but I had to give it a try." He rolled down the window and looked at the ground below. "I don't suppose there is a way to get some traction under these tires."

Christine shook her head. "Not unless you have something in the truck. Everything outside will be soaking wet."

Wyatt pulled his phone out and clicked a few buttons. "We're in a dead zone."

"There's a farmhouse just past those rocks around that bend. Old man Denton will help us out."

More approaching dark clouds indicated that they were not past the worst of the storm, but it had let up for the moment. Wyatt glanced through the rear windshield, regretting that they may have missed their chance to find out what Champlain was up to. "Why don't you wait here in the truck where it's warm and dry and I'll go get help?"

Christine slipped into the windbreaker she had taken off earlier. "A stranger knocking on Denton's door is only going to make him suspicious. It would be best if I went with you." She pushed open the truck door.

Wyatt shrugged. When Christine made up her mind about something, he knew it would be futile to argue. He grabbed his own jacket and stepped out onto the muddy bank. Though thunder boomed in the distance, the rainfall had lightened up. Christine walked beside Wyatt with her arms crossed.

He didn't see smoke rising in the air or anything

that indicated a farmhouse was close by. "How far did you say it was?"

"I've never actually walked it." She turned back to where they had left the disabled truck. "I'm guessing it won't take us more than ten or fifteen minutes."

Rain fell at a greater volume as thunder and lightning indicated another wave of the storm was about to hit them. Like a bucket being poured from the sky, the rain came down in solid sheets, soaking both of them.

They rounded the curve of the outcropping of rock. In the distance, built at the base of the hill was a white house surrounded by several barns and corrals. That had to be another twenty minutes down the dirt road to get to the house.

Lightning struck a tree not twenty feet in front of them. Christine jumped and pressed a little closer to Wyatt. "Sorry, guess it is farther than I realized." She couldn't hide the fear in her voice.

He put his mouth close to her ear. "Maybe we should wait this one out."

"It would be just as far to go back to the truck as to make it to the house." Christine raised her voice above the downpour and rush of wind.

Wyatt wrapped his arms around Christine's slender waist and ushered her toward the outcropping of rock, which was barely visible through the intense rain. "We'll wait here, then."

They ran toward the shelter of the rocks and

hunkered down beneath a ledge. Both of them were soaked, but at least now they weren't going to get any wetter. Dark cloud cover made midday look more like evening.

Christine shivered.

"I can't even offer you my coat." Wyatt leaned close. "It'll just get you wetter."

"I'll be all right," she said through chattering teeth.

He dug through his pockets and pulled out a scarf, which he wrapped around her neck. "This is dry at least." When he dug into another pocket, he pulled out a half-eaten roll of chocolate caramel candy. "Chocolate makes everything better . . . Isn't that what you used to say?"

Light came into her eyes. "You remembered." She took the chocolate with trembling hands.

"You're really cold." He grabbed her hands and held them for a moment. "You're dry underneath, aren't you?"

"Mostly." She nodded and slipped out of her coat. After taking off his own wet coat, he held up his arm, indicating that she should let him hold her.

She hesitated.

"Strictly for warmth," he added. She leaned toward him, and he wrapped his arm around her, being careful not to hold her too tight lest he hurt her injured shoulder. Slowly her shivering subsided.

"You've got no meat on your bones. That's why you shiver so easily." A memory flashed through his head of them doing cold-weather training. No matter how many layers Christine put on, she was perpetually cold. The problem with all those memories was that they were tainted by the way he had treated her. She had done most of the work to make the relationship work as long as it had. Why couldn't he have seen that back then?

"Are you saying I need to eat a pork chop?" she joked.

"A little body fat wouldn't hurt." As he sat holding Christine, a revelation spread through him. He couldn't undo the past. All he could do was make the future better for both of them, and he did want to have a future with her. He'd known that since the fire.

"I eat plenty," she retorted as their banter fell into a familiar pattern.

Her shivering subsided. At first, she had stiffened against his touch but as the minutes passed, she nestled closer to him. Holding her seemed like the most natural thing in the world. The rock they were under provided about a five-foot roof.

He didn't want their conversation to stay in the shallow place of trading jabs at each other. He turned toward her. "Christine?"

Her face was only inches from his. "Yes."

His hand brushed over her cheek and then he

pressed his forehead against hers. His emotions were so intense, he thought his heart would explode out of his chest, but he couldn't voice his feelings. Words of affection had never been spoken to him as a child. They felt foreign on his tongue. Christine's fingers touched his neck. In the darkness, her lips found his.

He responded to the kiss, drawing her close and holding her tight. Wanting desperately to say what he knew she wanted to hear.

He kissed her one more time before they nestled together and looked out. The electric energy of the kiss charged through him. The rain poured down around them. Gradually, the fast rhythms of a downpour changed to a light pattering. Every indentation in the landscape had filled with water.

Like a faucet being turned off, the rain became a drizzle and then stopped altogether. Water dripped from the rocks around them.

Christine pulled free of Wyatt's embrace and scooted forward to look out. "I think we can chance it now. Haven't heard any thunder in a while."

Struggling with a sense of loss when she wasn't in his arms, he leaned forward and craned his neck to look out. Their shoulders touched. "Yeah, let's get to that farmhouse."

They crawled out from under the ledge. The rain had done substantial damage in a short amount of time. The road looked washed-out in spots. Mud and water were everywhere.

They walked the remaining distance to the farmhouse.

The long dirt road was bordered by fences on either side. As they neared the house, a burly man came out on the porch. He crossed his arms.

Wyatt hesitated in his stride.

The man's face scrunched into an expression that communicated hostility.

TEN

Christine had to take two steps for every one Wyatt took. When old man Denton came out on the porch, his face compressed into an expression that for someone who didn't know him probably came across as distrust or aggression. Christine knew that Denton was squinting to see better. He had needed glasses for years, but refused to get any.

Christine waved as they drew within twenty feet. "Hey, Robert."

Robert Denton waved back, but gave no indication he knew who Christine was. When they got closer, recognition spread across his face. "Howdy, Sheriff Norris. Quite a storm, wasn't it?" His look hardened when he noticed Wyatt.

Christine stepped forward. "This is Wyatt

Green, one of the agents called in to help me with the bombing."

The introduction was enough to sweep away any of Denton's suspicions. He held a hand out to Wyatt. "Pleased to meet you."

Wyatt shook the man's hand. "I'm afraid our pickup slid off the road and got stuck. Can we borrow your phone to call someone?"

"I can do better than that. I can roust Kenny out of the barn, and he can use the tow rope to pull you out. You two look like a couple of drowned rats. Kenny can handle things on his own. Why don't you come in and get yourself a hot cup of coffee, sit by the fire and dry out while I get Kenny lined up?"

Wyatt and Christine entered the house as the older man lumbered toward the barn. The kitchen and living room were one continuous room. The far wall had firewood nearly stacked to the ceiling and a wood-burning stove with two easy chairs facing toward it. The sparsely furnished kitchen featured a worn Formica table and chairs. Faded wallpaper and ceramic canisters indicated that the room had been decorated with a rooster theme.

Christine stepped across the worn linoleum to a stove where coffee percolated. "Denton makes his coffee the old-fashioned way." With a little searching, she retrieved two coffee cups from a cupboard. "This should warm us up." A look of affection smoldered in his eyes and teased the corners of his mouth when she handed him the steaming cup. If she had had any doubt about what the first kiss had meant, the second one had swept all that away.

She pointed at a container on the table. "I think the sugar is in that ceramic rooster."

Wyatt dipped the teaspoon into the sugar container and slowly stirred it in. "Do you suppose the storm changed Champlain's plans, too?"

The thought of their only lead drying up frustrated her. "Hard to say. I don't know why he was even headed in that direction." Christine wandered toward the woodstove. "I thought for sure he'd drive toward Placerville and the badlands beyond that." Christine sat down and leaned close to the stove. The wall of heat that hit her felt wonderful.

Wyatt took the other chair by the stove. "Given what we know, it seems like it would be the logical launching point for finding the camp. The helicopter searches haven't turned up anything. If we just had a direction to go from Placerville, that would be helpful."

Denton burst through the door. "See you folks found the coffee. I got cookies if you want some." Talking in a loud voice, he made his way to the kitchen where a cupboard door screeched open and slammed shut. He came back into the living-room area and offered them an open package of cookies. "Haven't had home baked on a regular

141

basis since my wife died, but these don't taste too bad."

Not three months ago, Christine had attended Robert's wife's funeral. The poor man had been torn to pieces. "Maggie is always baking up more than Eva and I can eat. I'll have to bring by some of her goodies."

"Now, that sounds really nice." Denton set the packaged cookies on the table between the two chairs. "You've been through quite a bit in the last couple of days. How are you holding up?" He touched Christine's shoulder in a fatherly gesture.

"I'll be all right." She pushed down the twinge of sorrow over the house. While she appreciated Robert's concern, she didn't want to revisit those emotions. Best to change the subject. "You haven't had any more trouble with those coyotes, have you?"

Denton laughed and slapped his leg. "Not since you came out and gave me a hand."

Wyatt took a sip of the coffee, allowing the liquid to warm him. Christine and Denton talked and joked for several minutes about the coyote problem while Wyatt listened, unsure of how to include himself in the conversation.

Apparently, Christine's sheriff duties extended to running patrol to eliminate the varmints and making sure widowers had home-baked cookies on hand.

The conversation had a jovial and endearing quality. Certainly wasn't the kind of relationships he fostered as part of his investigations. Maybe her job wasn't as action packed as his, but the sleazy informants he had to deal with in his job didn't hold a candle to people who would pull your truck out of the mud or come in the middle of the night to put a fire out.

Through the large kitchen windows, Wyatt watched a man who was a younger version of Robert come up the walkway. A moment later, he poked his head through the door. "I got your rig pulled out of the mud. If you folks want to get down the road, I can give you a ride to your truck."

Denton rose to his feet. "Just a second. Let me grab some dry coats for you folks."

After Denton brought out two heavy wool shirts, Kenny dropped Christine and Wyatt off by the truck and waved goodbye.

Once they were settled in the cab, Christine said, "Champlain might be long gone by now, but it wouldn't hurt to see what was so interesting up by where he turned off."

"If we're lucky, he had to wait the storm out just like we did." Wyatt pressed on the accelerator. The truck careened slightly on the mud-slicked road, but Wyatt was able to hold it steady. He recognized the outcropping of rock where they had held each other while the storm raged. The corners of his mouth turned up at the memory.

"Don't miss the turnoff," Christine prompted.

Wyatt braked and backed up. Now he saw the butte in the distance that Champlain must have been headed to. The tires slipped into the ruts of the dirt road as the truck eased toward a stand of junipers.

The forest grew thicker and the road disappeared. "I don't think we are going to get much farther without getting stuck again."

"We can walk the rest of the way." Christine jumped out of the car.

Wyatt scrambled to fall in behind her as she walked toward what looked like a trail. The stillness of the forest held an unnamed threat. His instincts told him that despite the quiet, they were not alone. He unsnapped the strap on his side holster. Christine's hand wavered over her gun, as well.

Their shoes made a suctioning noise on the muddy ground.

"Someone was here either during or right after the storm." Wyatt pointed to a pair of tire tracks that revealed a vehicle stopping and then backing up. "Looks like there is a second set of tracks. Do you suppose Champlain was meeting someone out here?"

Christine stopped. Wyatt came up behind her, placing a protective hand on her back.

She tilted her head. "Do you hear that?" she whispered.

At first he heard nothing, but as he tuned in to his surroundings, a sharp ringing noise became more distinct. The sound grew louder, then stopped.

Still staying close to Christine, Wyatt turned his head one way and then the other. Tension threaded through the silence.

Branches broke close to them. The distinct yelp of a dog shattered the stillness, and a black Lab bounded toward them, but stopped. He took on a defensive stance, growling with his lip curled back and his hackles up.

Christine made soothing sounds as she moved toward him. "This looks like Champlain's dog. Something has traumatized him." She kneeled down and held her hand out to him. "Hey, boy." The dog sat on his hind feet and whined. After she let him sniff her hand, she petted him. "There, now. There—" Her hand recoiled. She gasped.

Wyatt kneeled beside her. "What is it?"

Christine held up a hand coated with blood.

The dog licked Wyatt's face, but yelped when his fingers combed through his fur. "I think he's injured. He's not going to let me get close enough to figure out what made him bleed."

Christine rose to her feet, her voice ice-cold as she looked at the blood on her hand. "What happened out here?"

Wyatt held the dog's jowls in his hands. "Where's your master, boy?"

145

The dog whined and lay on the ground.

"If Champlain is still out here, where is his truck?" She searched around the clearing, looking for tracks or an opening where a truck could have gone farther into the trees. "Why would he go and leave his dog here?"

With the dog trailing behind him, Wyatt studied the ground to see if it would tell him anything. He saw a boot print in the mud. "Here, this way."

Christine ran to him, gripping his arm. An acidic taste rose up in her mouth when she stared down at the boot prints. The boot had left the same impression as the second set of footprints around the hay baler. The insurance photo of Dustin's accident was seared into her memory.

"Something wrong?"

"I'll explain later." She dismissed the coincidence. The waffle-print pattern was probably common to lots of boots.

"More footprints here. This one is different." The dog pressed close to Wyatt's leg.

The overlay of the waffle print over the smoother, less-distinctive print indicated that two different people had come this way, not together but one after the other.

They followed the trail through the trees. The land opened up and the high shale wall of the butte dominated the landscape. A four-wheeler sitting off by itself came into view.

The dog barked.

Christine detected movement by some juniper trees.

The dog's barking became more rapid and insistent. Wyatt took the lead as both of them ran toward the trees, finding cover where they could. Heart racing, Christine placed her hand on her gun.

When they were within twenty yards of where they had seen movement, a man in a hat ran out, spotted them and darted toward the four-wheeler.

"Stop," Christine shouted as she drew her weapon.

"I got him." Wyatt chased after the man.

The dog barked as he ran toward where the man had come from. Still holding her gun, Christine followed the dog through the junipers to a flat, open area. A shovel had been dropped beside fresh-dug earth.

The Lab's barking was feverish.

Christine stepped out from behind the trees to see where Wyatt was. A light breeze tickled her skin. No sign of Wyatt or the four-wheeler. The dog stopped barking and emitted a low whine.

A popping sound thumped against her eardrum. Rifle shot.

She dived to the ground.

The second shot broke a tree branch three feet above her. Christine pressed low to the ground, turning her head from side to side in search of cover. The dog's barking faded as he escaped deeper into the brush.

The third shot zinged over her. Shale rock from the butte tumbled to the ground. At least now she knew what direction the shots were coming from. She had to find cover. The next shot was likely to go right through her.

More shots were fired, but these hit points around the curve of the butte. Had the shooter lost his mind? She was exposed. All he needed to do was sight in and shoot, and she'd be a dead woman.

She belly-crawled closer to the steep wall of the butte. A brief pounding of footsteps and Wyatt's voice was in her ear as he grabbed the back of her shirt. "Rocks, over here, now."

He must have taken fire on his run back to her. That's what the off-target shots were about. They scrambled toward the boulders. Wyatt braced an arm around her waist and pulled her to safety. He dived in beside her, breathless from the chase.

A bullet zinged over the top of the rock. Christine cringed. "We can't stay here forever."

Wyatt gulped in air. "We'll be exposed if we try to run to the truck."

Christine peered around the rock just in time to catch the glint of metal from a rifle as the shooter moved closer, taking cover behind the brush. The rock was too small to provide complete cover. She eased nearer to Wyatt. They were running out of time. It was only a matter of minutes before the shooter lined up a clean shot on one of them.

Wyatt's hand wavered over his pistol.

"He's not going to get close enough for us to get any degree of accuracy with a handgun," Christine said.

"We're out of options. Stay low. Make a run for the truck," Wyatt commanded.

Fear seized Christine's heart. She couldn't move.

Wyatt pressed his hands against her cheeks and looked directly into her eyes. "Are you with me?"

She nodded even as her heart beat out a frantic rhythm.

"Let me stay on the shooter's side. Stay as low as you can without losing speed." He pointed toward a mound of dirt that was higher than the flat prairie around it—not exactly solid protection from a flying bullet, but it would have to do.

Shots zinged through the air as they crouched and raced toward the first point.

They lay flat on the ground behind the mound of earth. Their legs were exposed to the shooter. "Once the trees thicken up, he's not going to be able to get a clean shot. Keep looking at the trees, Christine."

Wyatt pulled Christine to her feet. Another shot assaulted them, stirring up the ground in front of them. Christine stuttered in her step.

"Keep moving." Wyatt pulled her toward the safety of the trees.

They ran into the forest and then to the truck. Wyatt yanked open the driver's side door and ushered Christine in. He started the engine. The windshield shattered. Christine screamed. Wyatt pulled her to the seat of the truck. He crouched low behind the wheel, shifted into Reverse and backed the truck down the muddy road.

Wheezing in air, Christine pulled his cell phone off his belt. "They were burying something out there. Did you get a look at the guy you chased? Was it Champlain?"

"I never got close enough to see. He took off." Wyatt cranked the wheel. The truck swung around onto the main road. "I think the shooter was a different guy. Couldn't see him, either."

She stared at the cell-phone panel. "We still don't have any cell reception." Christine looked out the front window, which was still intact but was a web of broken glass. She waited for her heartbeat to return to normal. She glanced over at Wyatt, remembering what the other agents had said about him. *If you are ever in a gun battle, Wyatt Green is the one you want to be with.* "Thanks, you saved my bacon back there."

"I'll always have your back." The look of affection on his face changed to one of horror as he lifted his gaze past her shoulder. "Down, down."

She slammed her cheek against the seat of the truck. "What did you see?"

Wyatt pressed the accelerator, and the truck careened on the muddy road. "He's climbed to the top of the butte. He's taking aim."

Christine pressed her face against the rough fabric of the truck seat. Wyatt's hand hovered protectively over her head and then rested on her shoulder.

"We've got to be out of range by now." Her voice was shaking. How much longer would this go on?

He glanced over his shoulder. "He's still up there. Let's not take any chances." Wyatt's expression was one of calm concentration as he increased the truck's speed.

Christine felt as though her bones had been shaken from the inside. "Certainly takes a lot to rattle you."

"It's my job. It's what I do. Is there a house around here where we could make a call and get the ball rolling on what was going on out there? Maybe even catch the shooter if we had backup."

Christine scrambled to process what Wyatt was asking.

He drove around a curve, checking the rear-view mirror. "He's disappeared. Not even a trained sniper could make a shot at this distance."

Christine eased herself into a sitting position. Still crouching, she peered through the window to get a bearing on where they were at. Her mind went blank. "I think there is—" What was wrong with her? She knew this part of the country like the back of her hand. She pressed against Wyatt's shoulder. "Give me minute."

"Hey, what's going on?" His voice flooded with sympathy. "That really shook you up, didn't it?"

"All of this is starting to get to me. Being the sheriff of a rural county doesn't lend itself to this much excitement in just a few days."

He slowed the truck and wrapped his arm around her. She melted into the safety of his hug.

"You're really shaking." He stopped the truck and gathered her into a soft embrace. Christine rested her head against Wyatt's hard chest. He stroked her hair.

"Better?"

She nodded and pulled back to look into his eyes. "I could get used to that—not the shooting, but the being held."

His dark-eyed gaze held sincerity that made her feel warm all over. "Could you?" He swallowed hard, his Adam's apple moving up and down.

She nodded and reached out to touch the stubble on his face.

"Being an agent again doesn't appeal to you, though?"

The question caught her by surprise. He had just assumed if they were together, she'd rejoin the agency. "I've had enough excitement for a lifetime. Besides, my home is here now." Christine didn't pull away, but her hand dropped to his chest.

Disappointment clouded Wyatt's expression. "I guess I hadn't thought about that." He pulled free of the hug and shifted the truck back into Drive.

She hadn't thought about it, either. Finding comfort in his arms had felt so right. Wyatt may have changed for the better, but their worlds had drifted far apart in ten years.

The truck rolled down the road as a heavy silence descended.

Christine took in a deep breath. Her mind cleared. The bone-shaking fear of nearly dying subsided. She pointed through the window. "If you take the road on the left, there is a little yellow house. The lady who lives there is a widow. She'll be glad to let us use the phone, and she'll probably want to feed us, too."

"Everybody wants to feed the sheriff," Wyatt teased.

"It's a job perk." Christine appreciated his effort at lightening the mood.

"You've got lots of job perks." Wyatt got a faraway look in his eyes. "What I mean is, the people here love you and care about you. That is a good perk."

"Thanks. It does matter, you know, to feel like you are part of a community."

Wyatt tapped his thumb as though he were

mulling over what she had said. "We need to get back out to that butte, gather some evidence and figure out what those guys were up to."

Just like that, he was back to talking about work. Christine cleared her throat. "Mitchell and I can handle the preliminaries. We can arrange to send whatever evidence we find to Quantico if it's relevant to your case."

A yellow house with smoke coming out of the chimney and a fence fashioned out of sticks came into view. "Looks like Hansel and Gretel live there."

"You joke, but she makes the best cinnamon rolls in the county, and I am sure she will offer us some," Christine said.

As Christine had promised, the widow was more than glad to let them use her phone and offered Wyatt and Christine rolls and tea before they headed back to the butte.

By late afternoon, Deputy Mitchell met them at the butte with the evidence-gathering kit.

Christine pointed out tire tracks and footprints. "Let's do plaster casts of all these."

Wyatt put his hands on his hips. "What I can't figure out is if one of those guys was Champlain, where is his truck? He didn't have a four-wheeler in his truck. He had a motorcycle."

"We're assuming that one of the guys we saw was Champlain." Christine leaned down and picked up a brass shell from a spent bullet. "He could have turned around and headed to who knows where in the time we were getting our truck pulled out of the mud."

"There are at least two sets of tire tracks here in addition to ours." Wyatt shone the light along the ground. "We could do impressions of these footprints, as well." He turned to Deputy Mitchell. "I don't suppose Champlain showed up at his house?"

Mitchell shook her head. "He never went back to his house." She pulled the wood frame out of the sheriff's vehicle that she would use to pour the plaster in. "My friend at The Trading Post in Placerville said he hasn't come by there, either."

A shiver ran down Christine's spine. Things were not looking good for Champlain. "Mitchell, if you've got this under control, Wyatt and I will hike back to where that fresh earth was turned up and see if we can find more of these bullet shells and take some photographs."

Christine leaned down and picked up another piece of brass. This one from a different-caliber bullet than the first one she had found. "Not all of this is connected to the crime scene. People might be coming out here for shooting practice."

Wyatt held out an evidence bag for her. "Got to collect it all."

With the memory of having been shot at still churning in her mind, Christine stayed close to Wyatt. She recognized the rocks and mounds of earth they had dived behind to escape. She tilted her head toward the top of the butte. Her heart skipped a beat. Were they still being watched now?

As if he read her mind, Wyatt pressed closer to her. "I doubt he stuck around. He had to know we'd come back here."

Christine shone the light around the area where a mound of fresh earth rested beside the empty hole. "Looks like he had time to dig up whatever he had buried here."

Wyatt's gaze trailed slowly over the hole. "There's nothing here."

A glint of metal caught Christine's eye as she shone the flashlight around. She jumped into the hole for a closer look. "Wait a minute. What is this?"

Wyatt watched as Christine bent over and cleared dirt away with her fingers. She held up a watch with a broken band.

Wyatt had begun to examine the rocks around the hole. "There's blood on these rocks."

Christine voiced the thought that had been crashing through her head. "Maybe what the shooter came back for was a body." And maybe that body was Champlain's.

ELEVEN

Wyatt took the evidence bag that Christine had just placed the watch in. "So you think something happened to Champlain?"

"All the evidence points to the camp being on one of the roads that leads out of Placerville. He was all packed up to leave town. I think he was meeting someone here for whatever reason and then heading toward Placerville."

Wyatt held a hand out to help Christine get out of the hole. "But when he gets here, things don't go well and . . ."

". . . his dog gets grazed by a bullet and runs off or is scared off." Christine put her hands on her hips and studied the area around her. "This is not a place where someone would look for a body. If we hadn't interrupted them, it could have been decades before anyone found what was buried here."

"We can't do anything with that blood sample until we have a body." He laid the watch flat in his hand. "Is there someone who could tell us if this was Champlain's watch?"

Christine shook her head. "Who notices what kind of watch someone is wearing? He didn't have a wife . . . maybe another teacher he was close to." She snapped her fingers. "That basket-ball photo-graph at Vicki's place, of Champlain and Randy together."

They gathered up the rest of the evidence and loaded everything but the watch in Mitchell's car to be taken to the office. It was supper time by the time they knocked on the door of Vicki's trailer.

Vicki, still dressed in her waitress uniform, opened the door. "Yes?"

Wyatt couldn't quite read her expression. The look was somewhere between shock and fear.

"Vicki, I'm sorry to bother you, but we need to look at a photograph that was in Randy's room." Christine's request was filled with compassion.

The look in Vicki's eyes held none of the softness toward Christine he had seen on their previous visit. "Okay." Vicki stepped to one side and let them in.

The old man who had been watching television the last time they were here was not in his chair. The stiffness through Vicki's shoulders and the way she repeatedly brought her hand up to her face, suggested she was nervous about some-thing.

"The photograph is right where you left it. I haven't touched anything in his room," Vicki said.

They wandered down the hallway and into Randy's room.

"What is going on with her?" Wyatt whispered as he stood close to Christine.

Christine shook her head. "All of this has been hard for her. Every time we show up, it's bad news." Christine picked up the photograph.

Wyatt shook his head. Vicki was acting guilty about something. "For sure she won't tell me anything if I ask. But she might talk to you."

"Her nerves are probably raw from all that has happened," Christine said.

Wyatt pulled the evidence bag containing the watch out of his pocket. In the photograph, the arm Champlain had draped around Randy's neck clearly showed the same watch.

Christine's face paled.

He cupped a hand on her shoulder. "We won't know anything for sure until we find a body."

"What other reason would there be for the watch being in that hole?"

"He could have been the one digging the hole and it fell off," Wyatt said.

Christine shook her head. "I don't think so."

They walked back into the living room where Vicki sat. Her gaze darted toward them and then away. "Did you find what you were looking for?"

Wyatt cleared his throat. "I have to go get something in the car. I'll just be a moment."

Christine furled her forehead at him, but a slow realization spread across her face. If anyone could get Vicki to say what had her so stirred up, it was Christine.

Christine nodded in understanding. "Yeah, okay."

Wyatt left, closing the door softly.

Christine shoved her hands into her pockets. Vicki's emotional state did seem on edge, but maybe what Wyatt had seen was grief not guilt. "How is everything going for you?"

Vicki scooted her chair forward and didn't make eye contact. "Best as can be expected. I had to put Dad in the home today. With just me here to take care of him—" Her voice broke and she let out a sob.

Christine ran over to her and sat down in the chair facing her. She put her hand over Vicki's. Her heart ached for what Vicki must be going through as a mom. "What is it? What is going on?"

"I've lost him. I've lost Randy forever." Vicki shook her head and her eyes glazed.

A chill ran down Christine's spine. She hadn't considered the possibility that the blood could have belonged to Randy. "What are you talking about?"

"He called just a few hours ago. When you showed up, I thought for sure you were going to tell me he was dead." Vicki sniffled as a tear rolled down her cheek.

"What did he say? What makes you think he's dead?"

Vicki rose to her feet and turned away. She wandered into the kitchen and picked up a pot and scrubbed it with more vigor than was necessary.

Christine followed Vicki into the kitchen. "Vicki, what did he say? I want to find him as bad as you do."

Vicki let the pot fall in the sink with an eardrum-splitting clatter. "If he is alive, he'll just go to prison when you find him."

"I can't lie to you. He did participate in a robbery, there will be consequences, but he is underage. He still has a chance, but you have to tell me what he said."

Vicki swiped her hand underneath her nose. "He said he was back in Montana, but he couldn't tell me where. He just said he was sorry for everything that had happened and that he never meant for it to go this far. He put that bomb under the car because he was mad at Mr. Hart." She gripped the edge of the sink and bent forward as though she had been punched in the stomach. "He sounded frantic and upset and then he got quiet, and he said that he couldn't ever come back. I heard another man's voice and then he hung up."

Christine held out her arms and took Vicki into a hug while she cried.

After a long moment, Vicki pulled away. She lifted her chin as though she were trying to push down the pain. "I'm just afraid I won't ever see him again. His voice was so filled with fear . . .

it was like he was saying goodbye to me."

"We're not going to give up that easily. He's your only kid. I'll do everything I can to find him." She struggled to keep her own voice strong.

Vicki nodded. "I know you will."

"Did you recognize the man's voice in the background, the one who said something to Randy before he hung up?"

Vicki shook her head. "No. I couldn't clearly make out all his words, but he sounded really angry about Randy calling me."

She gave Vicki one final hug. "I meant what I said. I'll do everything in my power to bring him home safely."

When she stepped outside, Wyatt was waiting for her in the truck. She briefed Wyatt on what Vicki had said as they drove toward the sheriff's office.

Wyatt's cell phone rang. He lifted his arm. "Will you get it?"

Christine pulled his cell phone off his belt. The number was Deputy Mitchell's. "Go ahead, Deputy Mitchell."

"On my way back into town, Joe Sanders called me about an abandoned vehicle left by his junkyard. The description of the truck made it sound like Champlain's. Joe is over at his house, but he said I could go in and check it out. I'm here now. It does look like Champlain's truck, but there is no motorcycle in the back," Mitchell said.

The junkyard was miles from the butte where they had last seen Champlain. "That's a little strange."

Mitchell's breathing and her footfall as she walked toward the truck came through the phone line. "Sorry to give you the play by play. I just thought you should know right away."

"I'm glad you called. Joe doesn't live at the junkyard, does he? I wonder if he saw anything."

"I can swing by and ask him." A clicking sound traveled across the phone line. "The door's unlocked. I don't see anything in here that suggests foul play and—"

A sharp popping interrupted Mitchell. Christine heard a scream and a bang and then Mitchell's voice came from very far away as though the phone had been dropped, but was still on. All the breath left Christine's lungs as she gripped the phone. She could detect a metallic scraping, but nothing else. "Lisa? Are you there?"

Picking up on her panic, Wyatt rapid-fired his words. "What is it?"

Christine shook her head in disbelief, still not able to fathom what had just happened. "I . . . We . . . need to get over to the junkyard, right now. I think Deputy Mitchell was just shot."

TWELVE

Christine directed Wyatt toward a dirt road next to a field with a barbed-wire fence. He sped up. She struggled to get a deep breath. Deputy Mitchell wasn't just a good deputy; she was a friend. If something had happened to her—

The junkyard came into view. Buses, old trucks and piles of crushed cars peeked out over the top of the high fence. There was no sign of the sheriff's car outside the fence. Champlain's truck must have been brought inside the fence. Wyatt stopped at a metal gate. With her heart hammering in her chest, Christine jumped out of the truck and checked the chain draped around the fence. The padlock hung open and the gate was unlocked. She pushed the gate open and then got in the cab of Wyatt's truck.

Her hand was already on her gun when she addressed Wyatt. "Proceed with extreme caution."

Wyatt drove the truck inside the junkyard. Christine scanned left to right. No sign of the sheriff's car or Champlain's truck. It was a huge junkyard. Lisa could be anywhere. They eased the truck doors open and slipped out, dropping low to the ground.

Christine pulled out her weapon. A light breeze

ruffled her hair as she studied her surroundings. Crows devouring a garbage bag cawed and flapped their wings, pecking at scraps of food and each other.

Wyatt sighted in on different parts of the junkyard. He sidestepped toward her and raised his eyebrows, an expression that indicated he wanted to know what she thought they should do next.

She pointed toward a narrow road. Piles of scrap metal and old tires formed walls along the road, blocking out much of the light. They walked back-to-back, turning half circles and raising their guns.

Metal scraping in the wind made Christine nearly jump out of her shoes. They came out on the other side of the wall of tires and metal into an open area. A ramshackle building was designated Office and to one side Christine spotted the brown sheriff's vehicle.

They raced toward it, feet pounding on hard, packed dirt. Christine slowed as she drew closer, prepared to shoot if she had to. Wyatt came up behind her. She circled around the SUV. Deputy Mitchell lay on the ground. A bloodstain spread across her brown pants. Christine fell to her knees in the dirt beside her friend. Her breath came out in short, quick pants. She mouthed something Christine couldn't understand.

Wyatt remained standing and alert. Lisa's skin was as white as rice and cold to the touch.

Christine leaned close to hear what she was trying to say.

The words were breathy and barely audible. "Get . . . down."

Shock waves spread through Christine moments before a bullet hit the side of the SUV. A scream traveled up her throat. She flattened herself against the ground, draping a hand over Lisa.

Wyatt returned fire and then dropped to the ground.

"We have to get Lisa out of here." Christine twisted around. The shots were coming from the second story of two buses piled on top of each other.

A second shot tore up the earth by her hand. Lisa's eyes rolled back in her head. They didn't have much time.

Lisa patted the chest pocket of her coat and mouthed the word, "Keys."

Christine grabbed the keys and duck-walked toward the front of the car. Wyatt reached up and opened the back door of the SUV. He picked up Mitchell and placed her inside. Christine scooted to the driver's side, opened the door and crawled in. She stretched her arm to stick the keys in the ignition and moved to the passenger side.

Wyatt got in behind the steering wheel. Mitchell moaned from the backseat. Wyatt turned the car around and headed toward the front gate. Christine peered through the windshield. Oh, no. Champlain's truck blocked the gate. The driver behind the wheel was not discernible.

Wyatt slammed on the brakes, shifted into Reverse and drove backward. "Is there a back way out of here?"

Christine craned her neck. "Around that pile of appliances. I think there is another gate."

Lisa made a noise of agreement. The deputy was barely conscious. Christine climbed into the backseat and gathered her friend into her arms. "Hang in there."

Lisa dug her fingers into Christine's arm and managed a nod.

Wyatt cranked the wheel and spun the car around, accelerating before he was even out of the turn. He whipped around the wall of appliances. The back gate came into view.

"We're going to have to crash it." Christine wrapped her arm tighter around Lisa. When she looked out the back window, Champlain's truck barreled toward them.

Wyatt hit the gate at full speed. It swung open without much resistance. The broken chain dangled from the fence. With the truck still pursuing them, he cranked the wheel, causing the back end to swing out. He revved the engine and accelerated toward the main road.

Champlain's truck charged through the gate, but stopped as they reached the main road. Lisa felt heavy and limp in Christine's arms. "Are you still with me?"

Lisa let out a heavy breath and closed her eyes.

Wyatt increased his speed when they reached paved road. "It won't take long to get into town."

A gas station on the edge of the city limits came into view. Wyatt zoomed toward the tiny hospital, parked outside the emergency-room door and ran around to the back of the car to help Christine carry Lisa inside.

Shock spread across the administrator's face when they burst through the swinging doors holding Deputy Mitchell. He jumped to his feet. "I'll get a doctor."

A moment later, two medical staff appeared with a gurney and whisked Lisa down the hall and around a corner.

Christine stood in the middle of the sterile hallway, out of breath and dazed.

Wyatt came up beside her. "I'd say that was an ambush at the junkyard just like at the stock-yards."

Christine shook her head as a chilling numbness settled into her bones. "Someone really doesn't want us helping you guys. And they are willing to kill my deputy to make their point." She couldn't hide the anger in her voice.

The administrator returned a few minutes later. "Sheriff Norris, is there a next of kin we can call for Ms. Mitchell?"

The question sent ripples of fear about Mitchell's condition through Christine. "I . . .

oh . . . I should have thought of that. Her grandmother lives here in town."

The man put a hand on Christine's arm. "I didn't mean to frighten you. I just need someone to fill out the paperwork. In a town this small, I should know these things, but I've only lived here four months. I'm still learning who is related to whom."

"Lisa's grandmother is Elaine Mitchell. I can write down the number for you."

"I can just type it right into my computer." The man rolled his chair forward as his fingers hovered over the keyboard. "That way I will already have it on the form."

"Yes, of course." Elaine's telephone number was one she had memorized ages ago. She'd dialed it a thousand times, but at the moment her mind had gone completely blank. "It's programmed into my cell phone, but my phone is . . ."

Wyatt came up behind her. His hand rested on her back. "We've been through quite a bit in the last hour."

The man offered Christine a sympathetic smile. "Is she in the phone book?"

Christine shook her head and rubbed her temple. "I can't seem to think straight."

Wyatt ushered her back to the hard plastic chairs and wrapped an arm around her, brushing her hair out of her eyes. "The shock will wear off in a little bit. Just take it easy. Let's just sit here, catch our breath and see what they say about your deputy."

Christine nestled against Wyatt, grateful that he was here with her. The administrator made a quiet phone call.

They waited in stunned silence until one of the medical people emerged half an hour later.

Christine braced herself for the news.

The doctor laced his hands together. "She lost a lot of blood, but the bullet missed the femoral. She should recover fine. However, she is not going to be back to work anytime soon."

Christine let out a whoosh of air as relief spread through her.

"You both look like you have been put through the wringer. Why don't you head on home and get some rest?" the doctor suggested. "She'll be up to having visitors tomorrow."

As they left the hospital, Christine's mind had calmed enough for her to piece together the events of the past day. "Do you think that was Champlain driving his truck? Or was it Champlain who was put in the ground and then dug up?"

"Someone could have easily taken his truck from the butte. Whoever it was, I do think their intent was to lure one of us out to that junkyard for an ambush. What do you know about the guy who owns the place?"

"I understand that everyone has to be looked into, but I don't think Joe had anything to do with this. He is honest as the day is long. I think we would be wasting our resources to spend too much time investigating him."

It was dark by the time Christine drove Wyatt back out to get his truck at the junkyard. Joe came to the door of his office when they pulled in. Champlain's truck was gone. Christine apologized to Joe for the damage to the back gate and told him to come into the office to fill out forms to get reimbursed.

Wyatt followed Christine into town. He waved goodbye to her as she pulled up to the apartment building where Maggie had set up their new home. She let herself into the quiet living room. Jake rose to his feet and wagged his tail when she came in. It looked as if Maggie had purchased some basics for the kitchen and bathroom. A new pair of jeans and a few shirts rested on the kitchen table. Christine collapsed into a chair. The landscape painting and the linen tablecloth must have been thrift-store purchases to make the place look more homey. Her heart felt heavy. They would be able to make do here for a few weeks, but it wasn't home.

Maggie came out of the bedroom in her house-coat. "Hey, kiddo. Long day, huh?"

"Been having a lot of those lately." Christine kicked off her shoes. She tilted her head back and covered her eyes with her hand. "I suppose Eva is already asleep."

"Took her forever." Maggie moved to the stove

171

where she grabbed the kettle and filled it with water from the sink. "If she wasn't having trouble sleeping before, she is now."

Christine felt that familiar tightening in her chest at the thought of Eva having to go through all this. She'd give anything to protect her little girl from more pain. "Why don't you get some sleep? I don't need any tea. I'm going straight to bed." She rose to her feet and took the kettle out of Maggie's hand.

Maggie wiped her hands on a towel. "Your room is the second on the right. I got a good deal on some sheets and a comforter. And there is a nightgown for you."

"Thanks for everything you did around here. It looks nice." Christine dragged herself out of the chair and checked in on Eva before going to bed. The little girl lay curled up clutching Wyatt's coat and the stuffed animal she had escaped the house with. Christine soothed her curly hair and pulled the covers tighter around her.

She made her way down the hall and crawled into the unfamiliar bed. She fell asleep cocooned in the comforter with the smell of new sheets surrounding her.

Six hours later, she awoke to the sound of Wyatt knocking on the door.

THIRTEEN

Though her voice still held the grogginess of sleep, Christine looked fresh and rested when she opened the apartment door. "Kind of early, aren't you, Green?" She glanced around the room as though she was uncertain of where to find the clock.

"Is that Mr. Wyatt?" Eva came around a corner holding a worn-looking stuffed animal in the crook of her arm. The little girl had her mother's curly brown hair and button nose.

"Yes, honey." Christine gathered Eva into her arms and rubbed noses with her daughter before turning to address Wyatt. "I'm not sure why he is here so early."

"We have some stuff to deal with over in Placerville, but first—" He pulled a cell phone out of the bag he was carrying. "So I can reach you without having to knock on your door so early. The minutes are preloaded on it."

"Thanks. I need to get out to the house to find my phone as soon as I can. If I didn't leave it in the kitchen the night of the fire, it might still work."

Eva sucked on her finger for a moment and then popped it out of her mouth and pointed. "Is there something else in that bag?"

Wyatt couldn't hide the excitement in his voice. When he had seen the teddy bear in the drugstore where he'd gotten the phone, he thought it would be the perfect thing for Eva. "There sure is. How did you guess? Why don't you come see what it is?"

Christine put Eva on the floor. She ran to where Wyatt held the open bag. Bending her head, Eva peered inside and made an O with her mouth when she pulled out the plush bear. She stroked the bear's fuzzy head. "He's so soft. Thank you, Mr. Wyatt." She leaped toward him and wrapped her arms around his neck.

The hug surprised Wyatt. Eva's soft curls brushed against his cheek. An unexpected tenderness welled up inside of him. He didn't understand wanting to take care of her, to make the trauma from the fire subside. He only knew he had to do something to make her life easier.

A faint smile flitted across Christine's face before she straightened her shoulders and became all business again. "What's happening over in Placerville?"

Wyatt stood up. "Lisa's friend Darla over at The Trading Post called me because she couldn't get ahold of Lisa."

"Her cell phone is probably back at the junkyard," Christine said.

"Those two men who came in to buy things for a little boy are back. Darla said they will be there for a little bit while they are having some kind of repair done on their car, but we should go as soon as possible. That's why I woke you. I didn't think this could wait."

"We'd better get over there, then." Christine stalked toward the couch where her coat was thrown. "Eva, honey, go wake up Grandma. She'll help you get breakfast."

Eva nodded her head and pressed the new stuffed animal to her chest and then held up the ratty stuffed cat she'd saved from the fire. "Now Kitty Kitty will have a friend. Thank you, Mr. Wyatt."

The little girl's smile warmed his heart almost as much as her mother's did. Christine left the room to change. After Eva woke her grandmother, Wyatt watched her play tea party with her new friends.

Five minutes later, Christine returned wearing jeans and a shirt that was a size too big for her. "We'll take your truck. These guys might freak if they see the sheriff's vehicle."

"Agreed." As they headed out the door, he felt a renewed sense of hope after all the setbacks in the past couple of days. "Looks like we might find someone to lead us to the camp after all."

When they got into the cab of the truck, Christine laced her fingers together and stared at the floor of the truck. "Thank you for being so kind to Eva."

"It was nothing." He leaned forward to stick the key in the ignition.

She lifted her head and turned toward him. "It means so much to her . . . and to me."

He hadn't failed to notice the sorrow that colored her voice. Maybe their worlds were too far apart, but when this was all over, they needed to talk. Christine had shown enormous courage in raising Eva alone, but now he understood how much that little girl needed a father.

The drive to Placerville took less than fifteen minutes. When they stepped inside The Trading Post, Christine made a beeline for the blonde woman behind the counter. After glancing in the direction of the open archway that lead to the restaurant, she spoke in a low voice. "I'm Sheriff Norris."

"Oh, dear." Darla cringed.

The cringe was bad news. Wyatt struggled to keep his tone neutral. "Where are the men?"

Darla pursed and then flattened her lips. "I stalled them as long as I could. They ate breakfast in the café, and I had Willy hold their order just long enough so they wouldn't get suspicious."

Wyatt swallowed the rising sense of discouragement. "I thought you said they were next door getting work done on their car."

"I asked them about that when they sat down to eat." She bit one of her fingernails. "It sounded like they decided not to get the repair

176

done because it was going to cost too much."

Wyatt turned one way and then the other, trying to decide what to do. Darla looked as if she was about to burst into tears. "You did fine, Darla. You did the best you could."

"Lisa is my friend. I'd do anything to help her." Darla wiped off the counter with a cloth that rested by the cash register. "We went to high school together. I heard about her getting shot. Did those guys who were here have anything to do with that?"

"We don't know yet." Wyatt clenched his jaw. Why did it always feel as if they were moving one step forward and two steps back?

Christine asked, "How long ago did they leave?"

"Only a few minutes. I watched them from the window this time. They took the road going north," Darla said.

At least they had a direction to look. Maybe they hadn't lost their chance. "What were they driving?"

"A brown car. I don't know what it was, but it was one of those big, beefy cars for going off-road, and it was missing the back bumper."

Wyatt thanked Darla and then raced out to the truck with Christine.

"They don't have too much of a head start," Christine commented as she got into the cab.

"It's worth a shot." It was the only shot they had

at this point. Wyatt hit Reverse, spraying gravel as he left the lot. "What is on this road anyway?"

"I don't know this part of the country as well as the area around Roosevelt. Ranches and a lot of government land, I suppose." Christine shrugged.

The road ahead was visible for several miles, but he didn't see any sign of a brown car or any car. Wyatt let up on the gas as they passed a crossroads. "Could they have turned off?"

"Maybe, but I think the smart thing to do is to keep to the main road. Even if we can't find the car, let's just see where this road takes us."

After driving for a while, Wyatt pointed at the long stretch of road in front of them. "Okay, either they turned off somewhere or they were abducted by UFOs. I can see for miles in this direction and there is nobody on this road."

"Let's just keep driving." Christine stared out the window at the cattle grazing. "We should have done this right after I told you about spotting Champlain here."

"You said there were three roads leading out from Placerville. That's a lot of road to cover. At least now we know which way they went."

They drove by a trailer with a barn beside it, grain silo and several abandoned cars nearly hidden by tall grass. Beyond that, the journey was broken up by the occasional cow at a watering hole. They encountered only one other car headed back toward Placerville.

Wyatt tried to ignore the feeling of futility. That nagging thought that they were wasting precious time. There just had to be a connection to Placerville. Too much had happened there to dismiss it as coincidence. "Do you think Darla was mistaken about the road they took?"

Christine shook her head. "She was pretty serious about helping out and playing the role of detective."

A newer-looking house came into view about a mile off the main road, visible because of the flatness of the landscape. "This guy sure lives out in the boonies."

It was only the second house they had seen since they'd left Placerville. As they drew closer, he saw an old barn and a recently constructed building that looked like an oversize garage, set back from and on either side of the house.

Wyatt leaned forward on the steering wheel. "Do you know the guy who lives here?"

"I haven't met him, but he moved in maybe a year ago. This is his second home. His name is Charlie someone. Comes up here from California to hunt and brings lots of friends with him."

"You know quite a bit about Charlie What's-His-Face for never having met him," Wyatt said.

"This county has a low population density. When someone new shows up, everybody talks. I knew he lived out this way. I just didn't realize it was on this road. But that has to be the place everyone was talking about a while ago. That big, new building is an airplane hangar."

"We came all this way. Why don't we stop and ask him what kind of traffic he's seen on this road? Maybe he's seen the brown car Darla described." Wyatt turned onto the stretch of dirt road that led to the house. In the corral by the barn, five horses munched on hay and rested. Wyatt whistled when he looked in the direction of the airplane hangar. "Pretty fancy."

"The airplane isn't just to show off his wealth. In the winter, this far away from civilization sometimes the only way you can get in and out is to fly."

Wyatt brought the truck to a stop in front of the stone house with the big porch. Both of them got out. Christine knocked on the door and waited.

She pointed at the beaten-down compact car parked in the driveway. "Does something feel off to you here?"

"You mean he's home, but he's not answering the door," Wyatt suggested.

"Maybe he took his airplane somewhere. It doesn't look like he has any other mode of transportation."

"I'll go check." Wyatt walked toward the hangar.

Christine stepped off the porch. She crossed her arms and watched Wyatt saunter toward the hangar. The sun reflected off his coal-dark hair as he walked with that confident, even stride that he had. She'd been unprepared for the mixture of affection and confusion she felt when he'd given Eva the bear. Seeing them together had made her realize how much Eva needed a father.

Wyatt disappeared around the other side of the huge metal building. Christine wandered over to the garage and peered inside. A collection of tools was organized on a peg board. There was no car inside the immaculately kept garage. When she glanced across the yard, Wyatt had come back around the corner and was peering into the windows of the hangar. She wandered around to the barn. The door was unlocked. "Hello, is anyone here?"

A musty smell greeted her as she stared into the barn's dark interior. Saddles, bridles and saddle blankets were heaped in a pile in a corner.

Christine's feet crunched on the gravel as she walked around to the other side of the garage. A car was parked in the trees nearly hidden by the foliage. That was an odd place to park a car. Maybe it was out of commission. She walked over to the car, which turned out to be a newer-model Cadillac. The car had picked up some dust from being driven on the dirt road, but otherwise looked as if it had been taken care of.

She straightened her spine as an eerie silence settled around her.

Someone is here. I can feel it.

She jumped at a flash of movement in the trees, her hand going immediately to her gun.

She drew her weapon. "Sheriff Norris here. Please come out." She scanned the trees. A branch on a tree wavered in the wind, but she could detect no other signs of life.

Wyatt came up behind her and rested a hand on her shoulder. "What is it?"

"I don't know." Christine studied the area where she had seen movement. "It was probably just a deer."

His hand brushed the back of her upper arm. "All the same, we better check it out."

They advanced with their weapons drawn and Wyatt taking the lead. Christine's heart raged in her chest as they drew close to the second stand of trees. Both of them circled around and searched the surrounding area.

Christine exhaled and let her gun fall beside her thigh. "I don't see anyone."

"But somebody was here." Wyatt pointed at the tire tracks that must have been made when it had rained so hard and had now dried.

"What did you find in the hangar?"

Wyatt shook his head as they made their way back up to the driveway. "The plane is in there and it's locked up. There were slicing marks on the padlock like somebody tried to cut it off."

"Stealing a plane would be quite an under-taking. Did you notice anything else?"

"There's a gas pump on the other side of the hangar."

"That's not unusual. This far out of town, Charlie probably has some gas brought in. I would guess Charlie has a supply of fuel for the plane, too." Still unable to shake that feeling of being watched, Christine stood beside Wyatt and stared at the homestead. "Do you think the guys in that brown car were our last chance before they try to find a way to get Lansky and his kid out without being spotted?"

Wyatt looked around. "They know we are snooping around. That's why they went after Mitchell and Cranson. But if the men in the car are still coming in for supplies, it means the camp is out here somewhere and Lansky figures he's safer there than if he tries to run."

They walked to the truck. "When we get back to town, I can try to find out Charlie's last name and give him a call. He might have reported an attempted break-in."

Wyatt opened the door to the truck. "I think we're close. I can't say why. I just feel it in my bones."

"I hope you're right." Before she got in, Christine stared at the horses in the corral as the hairs on the back of her neck prickled. Why did this place feel off to her? "I want to get back into town and check on Lisa."

"Maybe she can give us some more details

about what happened at the junkyard."

"Sure, we can ask her questions about yesterday." They could visit Lisa under the guise of
talking about the case, but the real reason she
wanted to go was to see how her friend was doing,
not to pump her deputy for information.

They drove back toward Roosevelt. When they
were within a mile of the city limits Wyatt
pointed off toward the east. "What is that over
there?"

Christine leaned across the seat to see out
Wyatt's window. Off in the distance, a plume of
smoke rose up against the high blue sky.

FOURTEEN

Wyatt swerved off the road to get to the source of
the smoke. He tore across the prairie keeping his
eye on the rising plume, barely slowing down
when the terrain got rougher. They both jerked
back and forth in the seat as he gunned the engine.

Christine placed a hand on his forearm. "We're
not going to get any farther in the truck. Let's just
get out and walk."

They jogged past some large boulders and
around a low hill. Both of them stopped short
when they saw the burning truck. Flames shot out
of the cab. A wall of intense heat hit them.

"It's hard to tell, but I would say that was Champlain's truck," Wyatt said.

"We're going to have to get a fire crew out here to put that out," she said, calling it in. "Someone was probably trying to destroy whatever evidence we might find in there."

"All the same, I can make arrangements to have our evidence-response guys go over it to see if they can find anything."

Christine examined the barren landscape. No sign of a house for miles. Chances were, no one had seen the truck being driven over here. "There are easier ways to get rid of a truck, like run it over a cliff. This smoke can probably be seen for miles."

"More scare tactics. They probably wanted us to know what they had done," Wyatt said. "Either some guys from the camp have come into town or someone in town is helping them and communicating with them."

Christine crossed her arms over her body. It was hard to think that someone she passed in the street or sat next to at a school program could do this, but that reality assaulted her over and over. They waited until the fire crew showed up before heading into town to see Deputy Mitchell. Wyatt made arrangements to have the truck transported to a field office that could go over it.

After finding a parking space, Christine and Wyatt walked into the hospital. Christine wrestled with what they had seen at Charlie's place. One of the things she had learned about investigation was to look for incongruities. Everything about Charlie's place was incongruent. The airplane hangar was locked, but the barn was wide open. There was a cheap-looking car in the driveway and an expensive one in the bushes as though someone was trying to hide it. The tools in the garage were neatly put away, but the tack in the barn was piled in a corner.

When they entered the waiting room, her insurance agent, Lonnie Depaul, came around the corner and ambled down the corridor. He walked with his head down as though he were thinking deeply about something.

"Lonnie, what are you doing here?"

He lifted his head and managed a smile. "My wife is back in the hospital. I was just checking in on her."

"Back in the hospital? What happened?" Christine's voice filled with sympathy.

"It's just . . ." His voice trailed off, and he turned away. When he looked back at her, his expression masked the distress she had seen a moment before. "Irene is a trouper. She'll be all right," Lonnie said with forced joviality. The dark circles under his eyes belied his casual tone.

Christine didn't want to be nosy, but something was causing Lonnie distress. "Are you sure?"

"I heard about your deputy." Lonnie shook his head. "So sad."

Whatever was going on with his wife, he didn't want to talk about it with her. "We're going to see her right now," Christine said.

Lonnie shifted his substantial weight from one foot to the other. "Did Maggie tell you? I called her earlier."

Christine turned toward Wyatt. "We have had kind of a busy morning."

"The adjuster is done out at your place. We couldn't determine the cause of the fire. You should be seeing a check here in a short time."

"Thanks for doing that so quickly." The elation she thought she would feel at hearing the news was short-lived. Now she was faced with the huge undertaking of rebuilding.

After finding out Lisa's room number, Wyatt and Christine wished Lonnie well and headed down the hallway.

Mitchell was lying in bed when they stepped into her room. She opened her eyes and attempted to sit up. She brushed her fingers through her dark hair. "Grandma just left a few minutes ago." She tilted her head toward a table that held flowers and a basket containing baked goods. "The ladies from my church have already been here."

Christine patted Lisa's shoulder. "How are you doing?"

"Lot of blood loss, I guess. I was in shock. The muscle in my thigh was torn up pretty bad, but I should be okay." Lisa let out a heavy breath.

"Darla called Wyatt early this morning. Those two men were back at The Trading Post." Christine briefed Lisa on tailing the brown car and described what they had found at Charlie's ranch.

Lisa placed her head back down on the pillow. "Darla would probably know Charlie's last name. She lives over in that area."

"We'll let you get some sleep. I'll check in with you later. And, Lisa?"

"Yes?" The deputy adjusted her pillow under her head.

"Thanks for being so good at your job." Christine draped her hand over Lisa's. "I'm proud to be working with you."

Despite looking haggard from the trauma, a warm glow spread across Lisa's face. "It's what we do, right?"

As they made their way out into the hallway, Wyatt handed Christine his cell phone. "The number for The Trading Post where Darla called from should be on there. I'll let you make the call."

Christine clicked through the numbers and then punched the redial button.

Darla's upbeat voice resonated across the line. "Hello, The Trading Post. How may I help you?"

"Darla, this is Sheriff Norris."

"Did you catch those guys?"

"No, but I wanted to ask you a question about a

man who lives quite a ways up the road we went on. His first name is Charlie. He owns that house with the airplane hangar."

"Oh, yeah, Charlie. Nice guy."

"What is his last name?"

"Benson," Darla responded.

"What can you tell me about him?"

"Like I said, he's a nice guy when he's around. But he is not here right now. Mostly he comes up during hunting season. Sometimes in the summer he brings guests."

Anticipation heightened as Christine asked, "Well, there must be somebody taking care of his horses. Is someone staying at the place?"

"I know there is a corral out there, but he doesn't own any horses. That was there when he bought the place. Far as I know, he doesn't get a caretaker or anything. He comes back often enough that it's not an issue. He just locks the place up tight as a drum. He might have someone drive by and check it once in a while."

With this new information, a theory crystallized in Christine's mind. "Thanks, Darla."

"Sorry I couldn't be of more help."

"You've helped me more than you realize." After answering Darla's questions about Lisa's condition, Christine hung up the phone.

"You've got that look in your eyes, Sheriff Norris," said Wyatt.

Christine tapped the phone against the palm of

189

her hand. "I think I know how to narrow down where we look for that camp."

Wyatt's eyes grew wide. "Really?"

She handed him back his phone. Christine couldn't talk as fast as her mind was working. "How hard would it be to get a helicopter to drop us in?"

"I can pull that together pretty quickly," Wyatt offered. "We've got agents waiting at the resident agencies, if we need to take a team in."

"I think it would be better for us to find the camp, make sure Emmett is there and have the team on standby. If you and I do some recon, we'll know if we are dealing with ten men or a hundred."

"I can put all that into place." His forehead wrinkled in confusion. "Are you going to explain to me what you are thinking?"

"As soon as I look at a map to be sure, but I think they are so deep into the badlands that no road goes there. They are using the horses at Charlie's place to pack in and I suspect they must have other drop-off points since we didn't see the brown car there."

Wyatt nodded. "So the cars that were at Charlie's place aren't his. People are dumping the vehicles there and taking the horses."

"They must be using motorcycles, too. Those were the tracks we saw." Christine pushed open the door to the hospital. "Dustin had some things he used when he set up hunting camps that might be useful to us. I'll just get one of the cars at the sheriff's office. Can you meet me out at my place in an hour?"

"Sure," Wyatt said. "Do you need a ride over there?"

"I want to say goodbye to Eva. I can walk. It's not far."

Christine watched Wyatt trot over to his truck and get in. The apartment house that had become their temporary home was only a few blocks from the hospital. Eva and Maggie were playing in the yard with Jake when she walked up.

Eva's eyes brightened when she saw Christine coming down the street. She ran to the fence clutching the bear Wyatt had brought her. Christine held out her hands and hugged her daughter close. "Hey, Pumpkin, how is it going?"

"I like the bear Mr. Wyatt gave me, but I miss my princess quilt and I miss Mr. Monkey." Still hugging Christine's neck, Eva pulled her head back to look Christine in the eyes. "Can we go out and get them? I don't care if they smell bad."

Christine felt as though her heart had splintered into a thousand pieces. This was so much for a little girl to deal with. "Oh, Sugar, I don't know." She smoothed Eva's curls. "Tell you what. I have to go out there today. I'll see what I can save, but no promises."

Maggie rose from the lawn chair she'd been

sitting on and stuffed her hands into the pockets of her coat. "You going back out to the ranch?"

"I have to go get some of Dustin's things. I think I know where the camp is. If I'm right, I might be gone for a couple of days."

"We'll be all right." Maggie looked up the street. They were two blocks away from the downtown shops. "It's been kind of nice being in town."

"Grandma's gonna take me for ice cream later today," said Eva.

"That sounds like fun. I'll call before we leave town, and I'll bring by anything I can salvage from the house."

Maggie touched her steel-gray hair and tugged at her ear. "Lonnie called today." Her eyes probed Christine as though there was something more she wanted to say.

"I know. I saw him out at the hospital."

"So, you are going to rebuild?"

"I thought that was the plan." All the work she had to do to keep the ranch going, dealing with her hired hand, Larry, and the upkeep weighed on her. Rebuilding would be a huge undertaking. Was keeping the ranch really what she wanted? "Now I'm not so sure."

"I've lived out on that ranch since I was eighteen years old and a new bride." Maggie drew her coat tighter around her as the spring wind picked up. "There is something to be said for

192

being able to walk downtown and buy your grand-daughter ice cream."

Letting go of the ranch would be letting go of Dustin once and for all. "I guess I have some thinking to do."

Christine hugged Eva and Maggie goodbye before walking to the sheriff's office. With Lisa in the hospital, her part-time deputy had been bumped up to full-time. The older man was sitting behind the desk talking on the phone when she stepped in to grab the car keys. She was sure she was leaving the day-to-day business in good hands.

With a strong sense of urgency, Christine drove back out to the ranch. When she pulled up, Larry's truck was in the driveway, and the door to the equipment barn was open. The fire didn't affect his ability to get the land ready for seeding, and it looked as if he had fed the livestock. For that she was grateful. It just seemed that as a courtesy he would have phoned and let her know he was going back to work. The few interactions she'd had with him were evidence enough that he was hardly the king of communication. Still, her suspicions about him starting the fire were not completely allayed. Like many townspeople, he expressed bitterness over the FBI's poor judgment ten years ago, and he indicated that he wasn't happy about her working with the feds now. Lonnie had said he couldn't determine the cause of the fire.

Dustin's packing and hunting gear was in the smaller storage shed, so she wouldn't even have to talk to Larry if she didn't want to. She turned her head and braced herself for a view of the house. Her eyes traveled from the blackened remains of the kitchen to the rest of the house. Her home. Her beautiful, safe home.

She couldn't face going in there, not just yet.

Christine pushed the car door open and stalked over to the unlocked storage shed. Dustin had left his packing gear stacked in a corner. She picked up a saddlebag that was dusty from having sat for so long. Her breath caught in her throat when she saw one of Dustin's old wool shirts neatly folded on top of a box. She picked it up, expecting to encounter a blend of soapy cleanness and fresh air that characterized the way her late husband smelled. She brought it up to her nose. A musty smell filled her nostrils as a wave of sorrow swelled over her. Of course it didn't smell like him anymore. She had to let go of him.

"Saw your car outside."

The thundering pitch of the voice caused her to jump.

Larry loomed so large in the doorway of the small shed that he blocked out most of the light.

"Yes, I . . . I had to come and get some things."

"Hope you don't mind. I got to get that soil turned over. Figure I would just come out here and work."

194

With Larry blocking the only way out, the tiny shed felt claustrophobic. "I have to get some things done, if you don't mind. I need to load this gear."

Larry didn't budge. "Yup, the weather don't wait for nobody." He stepped into the shed. "If you want any kind of crop at all, we got to take advantage of that rain that's around the corner." He grinned, showing his big teeth.

Christine lifted the saddlebag and headed toward the door—Larry stepped aside. Once outside, she turned to face him. "Please, call me if you have any questions about anything. I know it will be a little harder with us not living out here right now."

"I'm real sorry about the fire. That is a tough break for you and your little girl." He stepped closer to her.

With Larry, it was hard to tell if his condolences were genuine. Lack of emotion in the comment could just be because of his social awkwardness. "I don't suppose you saw anyone or noticed anything that day?"

"I was long gone by the time that fire started," he snapped, becoming instantly defensive.

She stepped away from him toward her car. "I know. I . . . was . . . wondering."

"Wondering what?" His words came out like a shotgun burst.

"You heard about what happened to my deputy

and the other agent helping out with the investigation. It just seems like a lot of people around here don't like us working with the feds."

Larry's face went gaunt. "It's hard for people to forget what happened ten years ago."

This time the pain in his voice was real. Her tone softened. "I know." Why did a single event have to define this town?

As quickly as he had shown emotion, he took on his defensive posture, squaring his shoulders and sticking out his chin. "I didn't see anyone around this place the afternoon I was working." His voice held a note of menace. "If that is what you're asking. Fires start by accident all the time, Ms. Norris."

"I know they do." She headed back toward the shed and stepped inside to grab more gear. "I just wanted to cover all the bases."

Larry muttered something about working for the sheriff and followed her to the shed. When she turned around after picking up a box filled with camping gear, he was blocking the doorway again. Larry narrowed his eyes at Christine. She watched his chest rise and fall as he took in a breath. An icy tingle skittered across her skin. Why was he looking at her like that?

"Christine, where are you?"

Christine breathed a sigh of relief. Wyatt's voice was the most welcome sound she had heard in a long time. "I'm in here."

"I got to get back to work," Larry muttered. "You're not paying me to stand around and visit." He turned and stalked toward the barn.

She hadn't failed to notice that his inflection revealed that her questions offended him. Maybe she had been wrong in asking them. Larry was a rough-around-the-edges kind of person, but he had never been in trouble with the law or expressed views that were out of the mainstream.

Wyatt stood in the yard dressed in worn jeans, T-shirt and flannel shirt. His dark hair was slicked back off his face. "Everything all right? What's going on with your hired hand?"

"I'm glad you came when you did."

She watched as Larry disappeared around a corner. "Maybe we should keep an eye on him."

Wyatt looked at her. "You think he might be involved with the fire or the other things that have happened?"

Christine shook her head. "Let's just say he is a person of interest." She carried the box over to her car. "Some of Dustin's old gear. I know a couple who owns some pack animals. I'm going to call them, and they'll meet us at a checkpoint and guide us in. If this camp is where I think it is, we can have the helicopter drop us off far enough away so no one is alerted, but that means we will have a bit of a hike."

"Good, once we know the location we can

bring in a team quickly and extract Emmett and Tyler. They won't have time to escape."

She cut a furtive glance toward the house as her stomach knotted. "I promised Eva I would look in her bedroom to see if there was anything we could salvage and I need to look for my cell phone."

His dark, intense eyes studied her for a moment. "I'll go through the house with you."

"I can do it. We're in kind of a hurry. If you want to load up the rest of this gear that would be great."

He stepped toward her and placed his open hand on her upper arm. "Let me go in there with you. You might think this is going to be no big deal, but trust me, it is."

The compassion in his face and the tenderness of his voice melted her resistance. "Okay, I'll trust you."

Christine took the lead and made her way up the stone walk to the front door. Wyatt stayed close behind her. She pushed the door open and stepped into the living room. The smell of smoke hung in the air. Everywhere there were signs of water damage where the fire hoses had sprayed. It would only be a matter of time before mold started to grow. The whole house was probably going to have to be bulldozed. The condition of the living room upset her.

But it was the blackened wall closest to the kitchen that made her back stiffen as a gasp escaped her lips. Wyatt placed a steadying hand on her back, speaking gently into her ear. "You okay?"

She took a moment to look for her cell phone, but didn't find it. "I'll just go to Eva's room and see what we can find. I don't think I am ready to look at anything else." The less time she spent here, the better.

As they stepped into the hallway, she averted her gaze from the kitchen. The toxic odor of burned plastic was stronger in the hallway. She covered her mouth and nose with her hand.

When she stepped into Eva's bedroom, the rush of memories from that night was like a blow to her stomach. She could hear Eva screaming. Jake's frantic barking pierced through her consciousness and everywhere there had been thick smoke.

Her legs became wobbly at the sight of the broken glass scattered across the floor. A porcelain doll that Christine's parents had given Eva lay crushed on the carpet. The princess quilt was pulled back from when Christine had yanked a sleeping Eva from the bed. Wyatt's strong arms surrounded her. She would have crumpled to the floor if he hadn't held her.

His voice in her ear strengthened her. "Let's just look for something we can take to Eva."

Christine walked over to the bed. All the stuffed animals, the princess quilt, it all smelled of smoke and would only remind her daughter of the trauma of that night. Christine brought her fingers to her lips. "She always has all her favorite things on her bed."

"We might have overlooked something." Wyatt walked over to the open doors of the closet. "Maybe something special got stashed away by accident."

Christine opened and closed the drawers of Eva's bureau hoping to find something other than clothes. With each drawer she opened, she felt as though the vise around her chest were being twisted tighter. It was only material things, but it was all a reminder of the life they had had together.

Wyatt picked up a cloth doll in the closet, smelled it and set it back down. He studied the room. "Something that wasn't made of fabric could be washed. Would that do?"

"She needs something soft to hold." *Just one small thing, Lord, that's all she needs.* Fighting off that sense of despair, Christine glanced again at the bed. Mr. Monkey was not on the bed with the other stuffed animals or with the ones that had been knocked to the floor when Christine had yanked Eva out of the bed. She always slept with that purple monkey. She pulled back the covers and felt around the bottom of the bed until her fingers touched something furry. Eva must have kicked it deep under the covers while she slept.

She pulled the monkey out. The layers of

bedding had protected it from the worst of the smoke damage.

"Victory," said Wyatt.

"A little fabric spray and it should be okay." As they walked back through the house, Christine was grateful that Wyatt had agreed to come.

When they stepped outside, Wyatt caught Christine by the arm. "Why don't you go get in your car? I just need to go look at one thing."

She stood by her car and watched as Wyatt headed toward the kitchen area. He stepped inside the debris and disappeared behind a half-burned wall when he kneeled down. He rooted around for a few minutes more before returning to her.

"You're still thinking the fire wasn't an accident," she said.

"My training in arson is limited. Lonnie seems like a nice guy. Maybe he just wanted to do you a favor and get the money to you quickly, so he didn't look real hard."

"Lonnie has been in business a long time." She had to admit Lonnie did seem distracted.

"The place is so damaged. I don't know if an incendiary device would be easy to locate. I think we could justify the expense of getting our arson guys out here to have a look."

Christine watched Larry emerge from the equipment barn and cross the yard to the pig shed. "That would probably be best." She'd already asked enough questions to get Larry riled up. The next time she questioned him, she wanted evidence. Even if it did turn out to be arson, anyone could have started the fire. Her house wasn't locked up. They had been gone a long time to church that night or someone could have snuck in after they had gone to sleep. In terms of access, though, Larry seemed like the most likely suspect.

They drove into town. Wyatt pulled up behind Christine when she stopped by the apartment building. Maggie and Eva were no longer playing in the yard.

She leaned into Wyatt's window. "They might have already left for ice cream. Maggie was going to try to make the day special for Eva to get her mind off everything. I'll just run inside real quick and check."

Christine pulled her keys from her pocket and went up the stairs. Jake did not greet her when she opened the door to the second-story apartment. They must have taken the dog with them. As she made her way to Eva's bedroom, there was something disconcerting about the silence. She placed the stuffed monkey on Eva's pillow wishing she could see her daughter's face when she found it. Eva had wrapped the bear Wyatt gave her in a homemade blanket.

"Wish I could be with you, baby girl. Mama has to go catch bad guys." She raced outside to the truck where Wyatt waited.

It was late afternoon by the time they met the helicopter in an inconspicuous place outside of town. Several vehicles were parked around the chopper with about ten agents waiting for them.

Wyatt took a moment to talk to his commander while the blade of the chopper spun to life, causing the wind to pick up. One of the agents loaded high-caliber rifles into the helicopter.

Wyatt finished his conversation, grabbed Christine and raced toward the chopper. He didn't let go of her hand until they were inside. Once they were settled in, Christine leaned forward and explained to the pilot where they needed to go.

Her stomach lurched as the helicopter left the ground.

This was it. They were going to get Emmett, break up the camp and bring that little boy home safe. Her eyes wandered to the rifles the agent had shoved inside.

Hopefully, without any loss of life.

FIFTEEN

Wyatt watched from the open door of the helicopter as the agents on the ground got smaller and smaller. Getting this close to completing an assignment always brought a sense of excitement for him. He could feel conclusion in his gut.

This time, though, he also wrestled with some anxiety. His stomach had knotted up when he saw the number of agents they had pulled in. They wouldn't know how many they needed for the extraction until they had an assessment of how many men were in the camp. Maybe it was just three guys—Emmett and the two men who had come out to The Trading Post—and a kid. He tensed. And maybe there were a hundred guys out there, and they were armed to the teeth.

The helicopter banked and headed toward the remotest part of Montana. Christine had buckled herself into a seat. Her fingers gripped the upholstery. Flying had never been her favorite thing. At first he could see cattle on the ground, but gradually even those signs of civilization disappeared.

Christine worked up the courage to look out a window. A moment later, she tapped Wyatt on the shoulder and pointed. Down below was a brown car nearly hidden by brush and the waning light. He could also make out a couple of motorcycles. Another drop-off station even deeper in the badlands.

By the time the helicopter lowered them to the ground, the sky had turned gray with the promise of evening. They waved the pilot off and stood holding their gear as the mechanical hum grew faint and then faded altogether.

"This is the flattest spot I could find for the

helicopter. The guides should be about a mile up that way."

Wyatt helped Christine heft the backpack onto her shoulders before putting on his own. He handed her one of the rifles and picked up the other for himself. In the twilight, they walked over rocky terrain and then descended into a grassy valley.

Both of them seemed lost in thought, keeping all conversation only to the essential. The rifle he carried stood as constant reminder of the potential for violence.

"There." Christine pointed. "That must be where our guides are."

Wyatt looked in the direction she was pointing. The orange glow from a fire gradually separated itself out from the rest of the landscape. They must still be far enough from where Christine thought the camp was for a fire not to be spotted.

They picked up the pace as they came to an incline. "Who are these people anyway?"

"Ed and Mary Ann Smith are the best hunting guides in the state." Christine was out of breath from the uphill climb.

They hiked at a steady pace until a makeshift camp came into view. Four horses stood close to a canopy. As they neared the camp, Wyatt could make out a man sitting on the ground and a woman standing beside him dressed in a hot-pink shirt.

The heady smell of bacon and eggs wafted toward them.

The woman walked out to greet them. "I'm Mary Ann and that is my husband, Ed." She offered Christine a hug. "I know you said you wanted to push on through the night, but we thought you two might be hungry."

Ed rose to his feet to shake Wyatt's hand. Both the Smiths had white hair and wrinkles, indicating they were at least sixty. Ed's grip on his hand was like iron, though, and Mary Ann moved with the speed and agility of a twenty-year-old.

Mary Ann handed them both a metal plate piled with bacon, beans and eggs. "The eggs are powdered, but they will fill the hole in your belly."

They settled in around the campfire. Wyatt didn't realize how hungry he was until the first bite of beans hit his mouth.

"Have you had time to think about where this camp might be since I talked to you?" Christine scooped up a forkful of eggs.

Ed nodded and scratched his chin. "You say they are packing in with horses and some motorcycles. The gas they must bring with them. If they've got horses, they must be close to a water supply and some grass."

Mary Ann stood beside her husband. "We were thinking somewhere along Temperamental Creek would be the most likely place. There are some flatter areas that would allow them to set up a camp."

"We'll push on through the night. Get a couple hours sleep and then keep going since time is a factor here." Ed added, "We have a couple hours before it's pitch-black. That will get us pretty close to Temperamental Creek before we have to call it a night."

Both Christine and Wyatt finished their meal in less than five minutes. With whirlwind efficiency, Mary Ann doused the fire and packed up the utensils that had been used to make dinner.

"I'll help you get your gear loaded," Ed offered.

When Wyatt got close to the horses, he saw that they weren't horses but mules. The full belly invigorated Wyatt. With instruction from Ed, he worked quickly loading up the saddlebags. Already, he saw how having Mary Ann and Ed along would make locating the camp go faster. He hated involving civilians, though.

Ed strapped Wyatt's rifle onto the saddlebag.

"I don't know how much Christine shared with you about what we are doing here," Wyatt said to Ed.

"She filled me in. You don't need to worry about me, son. After Vietnam, very little scares me." He patted Wyatt on the back. "I'll make sure Mary Ann is out of the way at the appropriate time, but she can handle herself, too."

Mary Ann gave Christine and Wyatt hats with

lights on the brim. She handed them both rain ponchos to put on. "We might get a little wet tonight."

Wyatt pulled on his mule's bridle and they trekked forward. Ten minutes later, a light rain sprinkled from the sky. The sound of their footsteps over the rocky and hard terrain was augmented by the nighttime silence.

"Got a flat spot up ahead. Get a couple hours shut-eye. Reveille at 0400." Ed placed his hands on his hips and looked at the night sky.

In the time it took Christine and Wyatt to retrieve their sleeping bags and roll them out, Mary Ann and Ed had set up the canopy.

Five minutes later, Mary Ann had also erected a small tunnel-like tent. "We'll sleep in here," she said to Christine.

Mary Ann pulled a sheet of plastic from her bottomless pit of a saddlebag and placed it over the canvas canopy. "Extra layer to keep the water out."

Wyatt crawled into his sleeping bag. The evening coolness and the sharp tap of rain as it hit the plastic mingled with the soft sound of Ed's snoring.

He had only a few minutes of coherence before he drifted off to sleep.

He awoke in pitch-blackness, his heart racing over some unnamed threat. His dreams had been of the possible confrontation they faced in the next forty-eight hours. He clutched at his chest where his heart hammered away.

He felt around for where he had placed the hat with the light on it and switched it on. Ed still snored beside him.

Some distance away bushes rustled around him in the darkness. An animal maybe. He slipped silently out of his sleeping bag and reached for his shoes.

Then he heard it. Faint and distant. A woman's moan, clearly a human sound.

After putting his shoes on, Wyatt scrambled across the camp to the tent where Christine and Mary Ann slept. Ed stirred and made an incoherent sound that resembled a question.

Panic flooded through him when he saw where a knife had slit the side of the tent. When he peered inside he saw the back of Mary Ann's head and an empty spot where Christine was supposed to be.

Christine had not had time to cry out or reach for her gun, though she had placed it within arm's reach. She had awakened when a hand holding a cloth went over her mouth. She breathed in and instantly felt lightheaded. She had the sensation of being pulled from the tent and dragged through the darkness. Whatever she had been drugged with slowed her reaction time.

Tree branches scraped across her face and sharp

rocks dug into her back. A scream stuck in her throat and came out only as a faint moan. Her captor pulled her along the ground for what seemed like an hour.

A harsh whisper broke through her bubble of incoherence. "This is gonna take forever. Help me lift her."

She was flung over a shoulder. Though it was dark, she was able to deduce that there were at least two men. Their footsteps sounded muffled and far away. Her head felt as if it was stuffed with cotton balls.

She was placed on a hard leather seat. Then a man sat in front of her. She swayed and then leaned against his back. The pungent odor made her eyes water. This man hadn't bathed in some time. "You better hold on or I'll crush you under the tires," the man said.

The bike started up and lurched forward. Her limbs felt as if they were filled with helium as she wrapped them around the ill-smelling man.

When she peered over his shoulder, she could see the other rider in this motorcycle's headlight. The first rider turned his head sideways for a moment. The brief glance was time enough for her to recognize that the first rider was Randy Stiller.

Wyatt's heart thumped erratically as he took in a breath to still the rising panic. He was no good to Christine if he fell apart.

"What's going on?" Ed sat up in his sleeping bag.

"Someone has taken Christine. They slit open the tent and took her." How far away had they been when she had cried out? How many minutes' head start did they have?

Ed jumped to his feet. "Which way?"

"I don't know." Wyatt swung the flashlight across the ground around the tent until he found broken brush and drag marks.

Mary Ann stirred.

Ed had gotten his flashlight out, as well, and followed Wyatt into the brush. The older man examined the ground. "Through here. This way."

They stepped over rocks. Wyatt aimed his flashlight up ahead looking for movement, listening and hoping for any signs of life. Profound dread flooded through him. What did they plan on doing with Christine? Who were they? "Does anybody live this far out? Could it be anyone besides the men from the camp?"

Ed shook his head. "I suppose a man could survive on what he hunted out here this time of year."

Then they heard the faint sound of motorcycle engines growing louder and then fading. Wyatt pivoted one way and then the other. "Which direction is that coming from? I can't tell."

"You get some echo out here." Ed pointed at the dark hills in the distance. "My guess is it is coming from the southwest."

"I don't see any lights anywhere." Desperation closed in on Wyatt.

"Too much brush and rock in the way." Ed had already turned back toward the camp and spoke over his shoulder. "We'll travel light, drop most of the gear here."

When they got back to the camp, Mary Ann was up and helping Ed lighten the pack load on the mules. She shoved a protein bar in Wyatt's hand. "Eat."

Ed talked while he tossed items out of the saddlebags. "You and I will go on up ahead, taking only the bare minimum so we can ride the mules and cover more ground."

Wyatt tried to loosen the tension twisting around his torso with a deep breath. Could they even hope to catch up with the motorcycles?

"I'll stay behind," said Mary Ann. "This is now officially base camp."

"Are you sure it's safe for her to stay here alone?" Wyatt unwrapped the protein bar. "I mean, they know we're camped here."

"I'll be all right. I can shoot as good as Ed," Mary Ann said.

Ed softened his tone. "If they were after Mary Ann, they would have taken her, too. Betcha a dime to a dollar this has something to do with your investigation."

"Why take her, though? Why not just shoot us in our sleep?" Wyatt buckled the saddlebag.

"That's not a question we need to answer in order to know what to do," Ed responded. "We just need to go get the sheriff before something does happen to her."

Ed had a no-nonsense way of thinking that clarified everything. The older man was right. The "why" of kidnapping Christine didn't matter. They just needed to get her back.

Ed stroked the mule's ears. "Liddy here will go like a house on fire if we need her to. You ride her. They handle just like horses, but they are about a thousand times smarter. They know enough not to run themselves to death and don't eat as much."

They mounted up and headed out into the darkness. They rode as fast as the terrain would allow.

Wyatt pulled back on the reins when he saw a flash of light.

"I saw it, too," said Ed as he trotted his mule past Wyatt's.

These guys must be connected to Emmett and the camp. Who else would be out here? If the militia knew that they had been found, Christine must be some kind of a bargaining chip.

"Soon as we have a clear location, I have a hostage rescue team on standby that is ready to come in."

"Temperamental Creek is pretty long. I would hate to have them dropped off five miles away from where they needed to be. Let's get some clear intel first," Ed said.

They came to a more open area and spurred the mules onward.

As they rode, Wyatt wrestled with anxious thoughts. He had to believe that they would keep Christine alive. He had to believe that they would find the camp.

The motorcycle headlights flashed again, trailing across a distant hill and then winking out.

"I think I know the first place we can look," said Ed.

The bike Christine was on stopped. Randy's motorcycle had fallen behind some time ago.

"Don't try anything," said the rider as he slipped off. He pulled a gun from his belt. Randy caught up with them. "Put the cuffs on her. She's come around now. She'll stay on the bike if she knows what's good for her. I'm going to radio the boss."

As Randy's headlight shone on the man, she recognized him as one of the bank robbers from Idaho. The man handed Randy the gun and pulled a two-way radio out of his saddlebag and stalked off.

Randy pointed the gun at her. "Ms. Norris, please put your hands behind your back."

Randy's voice lacked commitment. He sounded like a defeated, scared kid. Christine's thoughts raced as she struggled for the right words. She had only minutes to convince Randy to let her go before the other man came back. "Randy, why are you doing this?"

"I said put your hands behind your back." His attempt to sound forceful fell flat. The waver in his voice and the way he adjusted his grip on the gun told her he could be swayed.

She scrambled to find the emotional Achilles' heel that would break him. "What about Mr. Champlain? He's your friend still, isn't he? Couldn't he help you?"

Even in the dim light, Christine could see Randy's expression change. His mouth dropped open. His shoulders slumped. Devastation clouded his features.

Randy moved behind and clicked the handcuffs onto her. "Champlain is dead. He tried to help me. He tried to get me out. After the robbery, he said things had gone too far. He was going to turn all of us in, including himself."

"But they killed him," she said softly.

A gurgle escaped Randy's lips. "It's all over for me."

"It doesn't have to be."

The other man stepped into the illumination created by the headlight. The harsh angles of his face and the bulging eyes gave him a menacing demeanor.

Randy seemed to shrink in his presence.

"Quit talking to her." He spat out his words.

"Boss says we can head back to camp. We've thrown that fed pal of hers far enough off the trail. They'll have to backtrack for hours before they can find us."

Christine's hand curled into a fist, and she clenched her jaw to stave off the rising tide of hopelessness. Wyatt and Ed would find her. They had to.

They got back on the motorcycles and rode for hours. The first light of dawn rimmed the hills around them and they rode for a while longer. When they parked the motorcycles, the man pulled Christine off the bike and pushed her forward. The sound of a river rushing over rocks was close. Judging from where the sun was in the sky, it was well past lunchtime.

The cacophony of men laughing and moving around hit her ears even before they stepped into the camp. Once in the camp, she saw why it had been so hard to find. Trees on one side and a high butte gave them all the cover they needed. Though she could not see the river, she could hear it in the distance.

She had only moments to take in her surroundings before she was shoved into a tent. She fell facedown onto the floor. She'd seen horses and ten maybe twelve men and lots of guns. No sign of Tyler or Emmett. What if they had already left?

Her cheek brushed the nylon fabric of the tent as she struggled to roll over and pull herself to a sitting position. As she repositioned herself with the metal of the cuffs digging into her wrists, she could separate out one voice from all the others. She recognized Harrison Van Norman's rough bass voice. How could a man who had once called Dustin his friend sink so low? Footsteps padded by her tent from time to time, but most of the activity, the laughter of the men, the sound of a rifle being fired, was some distance away. Hours passed. Her stomach growled. Her shoulders hurt from being pulled behind her.

The tent door opened up and Harrison crawled inside holding a plate. She caught a glimpse of evening sky before he zipped the tent door shut.

"Thought you might be hungry." Like the other men in the camp, it looked as if it had been a while since he had shaved.

"I can't eat with my hands tied behind my back."

"That you can't." He held up a key and reached behind her back. His touch on her wrist was soft, almost tender. Once the cuffs were off, he rubbed her wrist. "That's better now, isn't it?" His voice held a salacious quality.

She pulled away.

She caught a flash of hurt in his features before his eyes narrowed and one side of his mouth curled up. "Same old cold Christine."

She studied him for a moment. "I was never cold to you. You were Dustin's friend."

Harrison shook his head. "You just never get it, do you?"

A realization spread through her. All the time Harrison spent at the house. The way he always lingered after Dustin had gone out to the barn to work on something after dinner. She'd been too in love with Dustin to recognize that Harrison had wanted more than a friendship.

Harrison handed her the plate, which looked like beans and some sort of wild game.

She smelled the meat, gave it a taste to try to detect a drug. It seemed fine. "So why do you need me? What are you planning?" She ate slowly while Harrison watched her.

Harrison waved his finger in front of her face. "Now, now, we don't give up secrets."

She could push him with questions all day long. He wasn't going to tell her anything. He settled in by the tent door, leaning on his elbows and crossing his legs at the ankle. The way he watched her while she ate made her skin crawl. She took a sip of the water he'd brought in.

Her attention was drawn to his boots. Ice formed around her heart as she leaned forward to get a better look at the waffle-pattern tread. The same pattern she had seen where Champlain had been killed and in the mud surrounding where Dustin had died.

She was in a tent with a murderer. It would have been nothing for someone to start the baler while Dustin's arm was stuck inside clearing an obstruction.

She hid her trembling hand behind her back and forced any fear from her voice, speaking in a cool, even tone while her heart raged inside her chest. "Did Dustin know about your radical views?" Was that why he had been killed or had Harrison thought he would have a chance with her if Dustin was out of the picture?

He responded with a raised eyebrow and smarmy grin. He leaned toward her, close enough for her to feel his hot breath on her cheek. "You don't need to know, darling."

Her vision of him blurred. She swayed. Heat traveled up her face and her hands became clammy. "There was something in the food, wasn't there?"

He chuckled. "We just need to make sure you don't get any sheriffy ideas. You won't be useful to us for quite some time."

She fell forward and was aware of her cheek pressing against the nylon for a second before everything went black. She awoke to the sound of voices and a splitting headache, not sure how much time had passed. She tried to move her hands but they were bound behind her again. She recognized Harrison's voice. The men were standing some distance from the tent, but she was able to pick up most of the conversation.

Harrison said, "We'll go out in groups of twos and threes, so they won't spot us from the air."

"Sounds good. The choppers will pick you up at the rally point and take you close to town." The second voice enunciated each word in a staccato style.

"You have about a twenty-hour window to get out with your boy while the attention is focused on us," Harrison said. "Every agent in the state is going to be busy."

"The collateral you picked up for me—" footsteps approached and then a boot kicked the tent door "—will help in our escape. The feds don't want another black eye, especially around here. No one is going to take any chances with her along."

Christine's breath caught. So that was the plan. She was going to be a human shield for Emmett Lansky to get out of the country with his kid. No doubt she would be shot when she was no longer useful.

"Do with her what you want once you are in the clear. After the way her Boy Scout husband set our plans back a year, I don't care what happens to her." Harrison all but spat out his words.

So taking her wasn't only a tactical move, it was Harrison's way of getting revenge.

The noises in the camp lessoned. Voices became more distant, slowly fading altogether. Feet stomped around her tent. She could discern the clopping of horse's hooves on hard ground. In the distance, motorcycles started. Judging from the snippets of conversation she caught and the hubbub, the group was packing up.

Enough light came in through the corner where the window flap was not secured, that she estimated it was early morning. The drug must have knocked her out for a long time. A day had passed since they had taken her. It was early Monday morning.

Christine twisted her hands. The cuffs were not coming off. They were too tight to slip out of. The tent was bare except for a blanket folded in the corner. She had no tools to unlock or saw through the cuffs.

The camp fell completely silent. A breeze rustled the trees and rippled over the nylon of the tent. The river gurgled in the distance. Her only hope was that Wyatt would find her.

Two men talked in hushed tones some distance away. She recognized Emmett's voice from earlier, but could not make out what they were saying.

She scooted back over toward the window to see if she could hear better. Through a small hole in the tent, she saw Tyler Lansky standing beside a man who she could only see from the knees down. The little boy held a plastic airplane in his muddy hand.

Emmett and Tyler hadn't left the camp yet.

Judging from the number of voices she could separate out, not many men had stayed behind.

She wondered why Harrison and the other men were going into town. Once they were on the run, they'd be harder to catch, and she would be more likely to die in a confrontation. How long did she have before they decided to leave, too?

SIXTEEN

Wyatt stared down from the top of the butte. He had seen only one man move away from the cover of the trees for a split second, but in the half hour that he had been watching that had been enough to tell him they were in the right place.

The camp would have been easy enough to miss if Ed hadn't been along with him. The man had a nose like a bloodhound and eyes like an eagle. Once they had realized they were being led away from the river, Ed had used his tracking skills to find the trail the men on the motorcycles left that led to the camp. They had climbed the butte to get a better view of the area and avoid detection.

The other agents were on their way in the chopper. They had lost precious time. It had taken nearly twenty-four hours to find the camp and assemble the team. Hopefully, he wasn't too late. He needed to get down there and assess what kind of firepower they were facing and radio back to the team.

"This should hold you." Ed handed him a rope. "I've got it anchored down good."

Wyatt repelled down the butte and slipped into the brush. He crept toward the camp. He couldn't hear any voices and didn't see anyone walking around. The only sign that anyone had even been there was a fire pit that had long ago been put out.

He belly-crawled a little closer until a single camouflage tent came into view. He was in the right place, but where was everybody? He moved in for a closer look. Several packs had been placed beside the tent. He slit the back side of the tent open and peered inside. Empty.

He heard voices coming from the direction of the river. Wyatt scrambled back toward a boulder at the base of the butte. He looked over the top of the rock. A man holding a rifle stepped out of the trees. The man pushed Christine forward. She looked haggard and frightened, but she held her head up. Behind Christine, Emmett Lansky came holding his son, followed by a third man with a rifle. All of the men wore gun belts with pistols. Plenty of firepower, but only three guys.

Wyatt checked his watch. How long until the team got here? The men had been stationed within ten miles and the helicopter had taken off as soon as he had radioed in a location. Chances were, if he didn't radio back with intel on numbers and firepower, they would decide to move in anyway and create a plan of attack on the fly.

Tyler Lansky wiggled out of his father's arms and ran off toward the tent.

One of the men walked over to a backpack and picked it up. "We should get moving, huh?"

Lansky checked the placement of the sun in the sky. "They got another two hours before they are set up in Roosevelt."

What was Lansky talking about?

"All the same, the sooner we get you to the border, the better," said the first man.

Lansky draped his arm over Christine's shoulder. "They'll be looking for a single man with a boy, not a family." He leaned close to Christine's cheek as though he were going to kiss her.

Christine jerked away.

"Oh, you're going to have to do better than that if you want to be my wife," Emmett said.

Wyatt nearly jumped from behind the rock where he'd been hiding. How dare Lansky do that to her? Alerted, one of the men looked in the direction of the rock, watching it for a moment. Wyatt held his breath and sank a little lower. He might have shaken one of the tree branches above him when he moved.

He crouched so low he couldn't see anything. The conversation between the men indicated they were within minutes of leaving the camp. They could still be captured while they were on the run, but it made things more complicated. The team would have to be advised of the direction of travel. If he tried to radio the team now, the noise would give him away.

Wyatt crouched down and waited. He had only a fleeting view of Christine, and what he saw concerned him. To run out and rescue her would risk everyone's life. He had to wait for the team. It would be an easy takedown with the rest of the men here. He drew his arms close to his chest, holding as still as he could.

The men had ramped up the conversation, shouting at each other. A gun was missing. Twice they ran past the rock close enough for him to feel the vibration of footfall through the ground. Wyatt put his palm on the radio, fearing that some communication would come through and give him away. Sensing someone looking in his direction, he turned his head.

Five-year-old Tyler Lansky stood less than four feet from him. His eyes grew wide, and he took in a breath that caused his nostrils to flare.

Wyatt put a finger to his lips, making a shushing motion.

Tyler slapped his hands against his ears and then screamed. "Daddy. Daddy. Daddy. There's a man."

The camp exploded with shouting and a shot was fired.

In one swift motion, Wyatt grabbed Tyler and pulled him behind the rock while he drew his gun. "Stay here if you want to stay alive. If you move, you'll get shot."

Tyler's face grew wide with fear. "I want Daddy."

Wyatt surveyed the camp, but saw no one. They must have all hidden when Tyler cried out. Another shot was fired, taking a branch off a tree just above Wyatt. The branch hit his shoulder. He had to draw fire away from the kid.

Seeking cover, Wyatt ran. A shot zinged past his shoulder before he could dive to the ground behind a log. Christine's scream splintered the air. Branches broke.

One of the men emerged from the brush, pushing Christine forward and holding a gun to her head. "Show yourself or she dies."

Wyatt's heartbeat thrummed in his ears. He took in a ragged breath.

"You got three seconds."

Christine's crying shook him to the core.

"One," the man shouted.

Wyatt peered through the trees where he was hidden. Christine's face was drawn into an expression of intense fear.

"Throw your gun out now." The man pulled back the hammer of his gun. Christine whimpered. "Two," said the man.

"Okay." Wyatt tossed his gun on the ground in front of him. "Let her go."

"Show yourself." The man pressed the gun harder against Christine's temple.

Wyatt stood up, holding his hands in the air. "Don't shoot her. Let her go now." Without turning his head, he assessed his surroundings. A small log that could be used for a weapon lay on the ground between them.

The man turned his head slightly. Lansky and the other man must be behind him hidden in the trees. "Where is the boy?"

"Let her go first," Wyatt demanded.

The man's mouth drew into a tight line as though he were mulling over his options. "Where is the boy?"

Wyatt's eyes met Christine's. The pleading desperation he saw there nearly made his knees buckle.

I'll get you out of here alive, Christine.

Wyatt felt his chest rise and fall with the breath he took in. He sensed that someone was moving in on him from the side.

Not wanting to draw attention to where he was looking, he at first turned his head in the opposite direction. Then he looked down and over. Ed was standing in the trees. He'd have the backup he needed. He couldn't wait for the team. These guys needed to go down.

Wyatt dived to the ground and grabbed his gun. He rolled for cover. Christine kicked the man behind the knee, and he tumbled to the ground. Wyatt shot. The man moaned in pain and drew his legs up to his stomach.

The second man burst out of the brush with his rifle aimed at Wyatt. Christine was having trouble getting to her feet with her hands secured behind her back. The second shooter headed straight toward Christine.

Wyatt shot the second man, and he fell to the ground. Wyatt scrambled to his feet, kicking the rifle out of reach of the second shooter. He aimed his gun at the first shooter and then the second. "Neither one of you move."

Tyler Lansky's wailing and screaming filled the air.

"I surrender." Emmett Lansky's voice came from the brush. "Don't hurt my son."

"Come out where I can see you. Hands up." Wyatt signaled Ed to cover the two shooters on the ground.

Ed moved in and helped Christine to her feet, then picked up the rifle and held it on the two shooters.

Emmett Lansky emerged from the brush, his hands in the air. "Just let me see my boy one more time. You owe me that," he shouted.

Wyatt couldn't quite read Emmett's body language. His tone sounded more demanding than conciliatory, and the expression on his face was almost a smirk. What was he planning? Tyler's crying had been reduced to whimpering.

"Give me the keys to uncuff Christine first." Wyatt adjusted the grip on the gun and kept it aimed at Emmett. "You can say goodbye to your son once you are restrained."

"I'm going to reach for them in my pocket." Emmett's eyes bore through Wyatt. He tossed the keys toward Ed.

Once Christine was free, she ran over to Wyatt and handed him the handcuffs. She leaned against him trembling.

Wyatt put the handcuffs on Emmett. "Tyler, you can come out now." Wyatt kept his eyes and gun on Emmett, but spoke gently to the boy. "It's all right, you can come out. Go say goodbye to your daddy."

Tyler emerged from behind the rock, tear tracks trailing down his dirty cheeks. He sucked on his lower lip and looked at Wyatt.

Emmett kneeled on the ground. "Come here, boy."

Tyler ran to his father. Though his son began crying again, Emmett remained stoic. He said something to the boy about being a man.

Without taking his eyes off Lansky, Wyatt spoke softly to her. "You doing okay?"

She nodded. "I'll feel better when these guys are in jail." Though she squared her shoulders and tried to sound strong, he caught the vibrato in her voice.

He appreciated her show of courage, but *he* wouldn't feel better until he could hold her in his arms.

"Tyler, do you want to come stand by me?"

Emmett rose to his feet. "Go on, son. Go over there by the woman."

Tyler swiped a dirty fist across his eyes and pouted, but he trudged toward Christine, who gathered him in her arms.

Wyatt radioed the team commander. He shut off his radio and looked at Ed and Christine. "We're going to have to hike out about a mile. I have the coordinates. There is a flat spot there where the chopper came down. The team is already on the move. They'll meet us half-way."

"I've got to take care of the animals and get back to Mary Ann," said Ed.

Wyatt slapped the older man on the back and thanked him for all his help. He tilted his head sideways and pointed the gun at Emmett. "Let's go."

Emmett brushed past Wyatt and whispered, "You ain't seen the last of me yet."

"Shut up and march," said Wyatt.

They hiked to the landing pad without incident. Still restrained, the prisoners were placed at the rear of the first chopper. Christine climbed in holding on to a solemn Tyler. She smoothed his hair and said something comforting in his ear, but the boy simply looked straight ahead.

It would be a long time before Tyler got over all that he had been through. Some of it would probably never make sense to him. In addition to the chopper pilot, a senior agent was in the front seat.

He patted Wyatt on the shoulder. Wyatt shouted above the roar of the chopper as the blade sliced the air. "Christine said some of the other men already left the camp?"

"Didn't see them." The senior agent shook his head.

Emmett studied Wyatt as though he were peeling back layers of skin. His eyes narrowed into slits and his mouth stretched tight.

The chopper lifted off the ground with a jerk. Noise came over the radio and the senior agent took the call. Wyatt couldn't hear what was being said, but at first the agent nodded and then his expression grew grim. He gripped the radio so tight his knuckles whitened. He clicked off the radio.

Wyatt leaned toward him. "What is it?"

"We've got trouble in town, a hostage situation."

SEVENTEEN

Christine's chest grew tight as she watched the interaction between Wyatt and the other agent. Something was going on.

She stroked Tyler's silky hair. When she gazed down at the boy falling asleep on her lap, she thought her heart would break for him. He had been torn from his mother's arms and now everything that was happening to his father was like an arrow going through his heart. So much confusion and so much trauma for one so young. While he slept, she prayed for him.

The helicopter touched down in a field not too far from town. U.S. Marshals had been called in to take Emmett and his cohorts into custody. Tyler's mother had probably been notified if she wasn't in town already.

There was a local news van. But what surprised her was that the number of agents had tripled from the time they had left. This was what they had been trying to avoid. Dozens of agents swarming in and taking over the town of Roosevelt would only open old wounds. This many agents was totally unnecessary. Christine felt her ire rise. She needed to find out who had made such a decision after they had been so careful not to have a repeat of ten years ago.

As they stepped out of the helicopter, Wyatt clutched Christine's arm and led her away from the chopper. Concern etched across his face. He placed his hands on her shoulders.

"What's going on?" She braced herself for what he might say.

"The rest of Emmett's group came into town. They let most of the students in the school go but are holding some hostages, including children.

When the word got to them that we had Emmett, letting him go was added to the demands they were already making."

Christine couldn't get a deep breath as fear filled every molecule of her body. "Which school?"

Wyatt took in a breath and squeezed her shoulders. "They targeted Eva's class on purpose."

A scream trapped in her throat as she shook her head in disbelief. "No, no, this is not happening." She pulled away from him.

"Christine, listen to me. We've got the best hostage negotiators in the world."

None of that mattered to her right now. She didn't care. Her daughter was in danger. Eva could die. "I have to go to her. She needs me."

He wrapped his arms around her and pulled her close. "I want to get Eva out as badly as you do." His voice faltered. "She's a very special little girl." He pulled back and looked at her with glazed eyes. "You both have become so important to me."

The look of love in his eyes pierced through her and calmed her. She'd never seen him this broken up before. "Oh, Wyatt."

"I know you don't think I could ever take care of a family."

"That's not true." She traced his jawline with her thumb. "I don't think that anymore." In everything he had done, he had proved over and over that he was a changed man.

He pulled her close and she rested her cheek against his chest. "Let's go do everything we can to get her out of there." His voice was thick with emotion.

Christine closed her eyes, relishing the safety of Wyatt's strong arms. A thousand anxious thoughts tumbled through her head. What if they couldn't get Eva and the other children out? What if this was a repeat of ten years ago and a child died again? The town would never recover. She gulped in a breath, drawing strength from his embrace.

He bent his head toward her ear and whispered, "Lord, we need Your help. Please give us strength and wisdom and peace. Please keep Eva and the other children safe."

Another agent approached them. "We're ready to go over to the school if you two need a ride."

The tension in the car was almost palpable as Christine and Wyatt and three other agents piled into a black Suburban. Wyatt cupped his hand over Christine's. The car rolled down Main Street, past the sheriff's office, the café and the hardware store. This was her town, her home. Would it ever be the same after this?

As they turned the corner toward the school, Christine felt as though her heart were in a vise being squeezed tighter and tighter. A crowd had gathered about a block from the school where the FBI had cordoned off the area. Deputy

Mitchell, walking with a limp, helped with crowd control.

The negotiation team clustered inside a van while a dozen agents stood around outside or helped with the crowd.

Agent Cranson hobbled over to them on crutches. "They've got a phone line to the hostage takers set up."

"What are their demands besides Emmett's release?" Wyatt asked.

"Their initial demand was money and a way out of the country, and they gave us a list of 'unlawfully imprisoned' men they want freed from jails around the country," Cranson said. "We pulled in a negotiator from one of the nearby bureau offices, and we've got one of the best in the Bureau flying up from Salt Lake."

"That could take hours before he gets here." Christine couldn't hide the panic she felt.

Cranson touched Christine's arm just above the elbow. "Our local guy is doing a good job. Right now, his questions are probing for weakness. Harrison Van Norman is doing all the talking for the group. Christine, you know that guy—what can you tell us that might be helpful?"

A thousand thoughts and images bombarded Christine at once as she relived every encounter with Harrison. Conversations flitted through her mind. The problem was that Harrison had been pretending to be somebody he wasn't the whole time she had known him. He'd even fooled Dustin for a time.

She stared at the school, focusing on the first-floor window that she knew was Eva's classroom. An idea formed. There was somebody else in there whom she knew well. "The weakness isn't with Harrison. He's a true believer. He'll die for Emmett. You have to get to Randy Stiller."

"The kid?" said Wyatt.

"Randy is not the one talking on the phone," Cranson said.

She had seen how broken up he was after Champlain's death. Only fear was making him a willing participant. "We have to get to him directly. He wants out, and he regrets what he has done. He'll help us if he is given the chance."

Cranson moved toward the van. "Maybe we can get him to talk on the phone."

"No," said Christine. "We have to get in there and find him and talk to him face-to-face."

Wyatt jumped in. "No, there is too much risk involved."

"There is too much risk involved in waiting," Christine countered. She gazed over at the towns-people who were watching. "Negotiations will lead to standoffs, and standoffs make agents impulsive."

Cranson and Wyatt exchanged nervous glances. Nobody wanted a repeat of what had happened ten years ago.

"If we can get into that school and isolate Randy, I believe he will help us get those kids out. He doesn't want to make things worse. He wants to redeem himself for all the trouble he has caused."

Wyatt looked at Cranson. "I think she's right. We take in four or five of our best guys and locate Randy. Get him where we can talk to him alone."

With her heart beating wildly from fear, Christine stepped forward. "I have to be the one to talk to him. I'm the one he trusts."

Wyatt studied Christine for a moment. "I can't send you in there."

"Do you think he is going to talk to an agent? It has to be me, Wyatt. Let me go in."

Wyatt's nod of approval came slowly. "Okay, we will give it a try. But you stay close to me, and the second I say we need to get out of there, we go."

"I'll go see if I can get the okay on this." Cranson hobbled toward the van.

"We'll need a blueprint of the school," Wyatt said.

"I'll send Mitchell down to the courthouse."

Wyatt looked around at the other agents. "I'll handpick who goes in there with us."

Ten minutes later, they had the blueprint laid out on a table in the van. "The classroom is on the ground floor in the corner. We can send in two guys this way and two guys from this side. It would be easy enough to have agents on the roof, too." Wyatt turned to the negotiator sitting at the table. "How many men are in there besides Harrison and Randy?"

"Based on what the students who were released told us, we are estimating between six and eight. One of the last students out reported seeing a guy posted here." The negotiator pointed to a stairwell. "Five minutes ago, a man stepped by a window here."

Wyatt studied the map. "Any indication where Stiller might be?"

The negotiator shook his head. "No clear ID on anyone. We know at least two of them are in the classroom." The negotiator wiggled in his chair. "I think I know how we can get you in there. They've already asked for food. We can request that they send an unarmed guy to meet Christine with the food. She might be able to see something, so we know the location of the men and maybe even where this Randy kid is."

Wyatt tapped his fist on the table. "That leaves Christine exposed. I won't do it."

"Wyatt, it's the only way," Christine pleaded. "I was in their camp. My gut instinct is that these guys would rather die than surrender. And if they are willing to die, they are probably willing to take children and teachers with them. Time is not on our side."

"I can't send you in there. I can't put you in harm's way."

She clutched his hand at the wrist. "This is part of my job. I'm sworn to protect the people of this town. You have to let me do my job."

Wyatt relented. "You stay close to me. I'll have your back the whole time. We move in slow. We get as much information about their positioning and numbers as we can."

Twenty minutes later, two men were on the roof and four had entered the school far from Eva's classroom, but moving toward it.

Wyatt turned off the radio he'd been using to communicate with the men he'd put in place. "My men haven't seen anyone yet. They must all be clustered close to that classroom."

The negotiator pulled the phone away from his ear. "Sheriff Norris, a man will meet you in the hallway outside the principal's office. He will be unarmed."

Christine held up a bag of food and drinks the café had donated along with two pizza boxes. "I'm ready. Let's do this." Thoughts of holding Eva helped her push past the fear that was making her tremble. Whatever it took, she was going to get those children out alive.

Wyatt followed behind Christine. "The principal's office is about two rooms down from the kindergarten room—am I remembering right?"

Christine nodded. They circled around to the

239

back of the school. The swinging doors squeaked as Wyatt pushed them open for her.

"You're going to need to hang back. The deal will be off if they see you."

"I know." His voice was wrought with worry. "I'll be right around the corner listening and ready." He kissed her, lingering for a moment before he brushed his finger over her lips. The love that went unspoken, she could see in his eyes.

Christine's footsteps echoed in the empty, dark hallway as she made her way past lockers and classrooms. She stopped outside the principal's office. If she couldn't talk her way deeper into the school, she wouldn't be able to gather any information or locate Randy. She glanced back to where Wyatt was hidden. She was confident he could get to her fast enough if they tried to hurt her.

From a long way off, she could hear approaching footsteps echoing through the empty hallways. Her heart thudded in her chest and every muscle tensed. Randy came around the corner opposite of where Wyatt was. This was a small miracle. She wouldn't be close enough to see into the classroom, but she could talk directly to Randy.

Randy made an almost indiscernible side glance, giving away that there was another man just around the corner. They had both brought backup.

"Randy?" The single word she uttered contained a thousand desperate pleas.

"You're supposed to put the food down and step back ten steps."

"Is . . . is Eva okay?"

"Just do what I say." His voice cracked and conveyed none of the toughness he had intended it to.

She set the food down and stepped backward. Christine fought off the rising despair. This far apart anything she said would be overheard. She had to find a way to break him, to get to him. This was her only chance.

"Your mom is heartbroken."

"Shut up. Leave my mom out of this," he commanded. He ambled forward and picked up the food. He set the heavy bag of food and water down as he repositioned the pizza boxes. "You need to leave the school now."

His voice contained bravado, but his eyes pleaded with her.

Christine took a step toward him. She couldn't give up this easily. "Please, Randy—"

Randy's eyes grew wide with panic as he glanced to the side. The second man burst out from around the corner firing wildly. Christine fell to the floor. A shot was fired from Wyatt's direction.

Pounding footsteps came toward her from both directions. Food scattered all over the hallway.

Someone grabbed her shirt collar and yanked her up. A gun went to her head.

Wyatt stopped in the hallway.

"You back off. You back off," said the man as he pressed the gun harder against her heart.

The man dragged Christine around the corner. She couldn't see Randy, though she had heard footsteps moving away from the ruckus. Her last impression of Wyatt had been of him standing with a look of unbearable agony on his face.

EIGHTEEN

Wyatt slipped behind a set of lockers and pulled out his radio. He squeezed his eyes shut and prayed for guidance. He had to think clearly. At the most, they had five minutes to take advantage of the disruption caused by things not going according to plan. He should not have let this happen to Christine. He fought past overwhelming emotion and images flashing through his mind about what might happen to her. He had to put a plan together to save her, to save everyone. He had to do this for Christine, for Eva, for this whole town.

Chances were, Christine would be taken back to the classroom. The men would feel disoriented; they might argue about what to do next. That was the window of opportunity the agents had.

He clicked on his radio. "Send in the rest of the men. Full assault on that classroom, from the roof and from the side. I've got the hallway door. On my watch, three minutes. Identify targets clearly before shooting. No children can be injured. I repeat. I don't want a civilian to get so much as a broken fingernail."

He ran down the hall and around the corner. A second agent came up the stairs from the opposite direction.

Just as he had hoped, he could hear men yelling as he approached the classroom.

The other agent moved to the opposite side of the hall as he peered around the wall. The yelling was coming from inside the classroom. A single gunman stood outside the door.

He checked his watch. Thirty seconds.

It felt as though an elephant had sat on his chest when the sound of children crying floated up the hallway. They had to save those kids.

He checked his watch again and nodded to the other agent. They raced down the hall. Wyatt hit the guard at the door on the back of the head before he had a chance to turn around and see them. Inside the classroom, he heard glass breaking and screaming, then gunshots. Another militia member raced up the hallway. A shot narrowly missed Wyatt's ear as he flung open the door and stepped inside.

More shots were fired as the second agent took on the man in the hallway.

Two agents had repelled off the roof and come in through the windows. One of them lay on the floor pressing a hand over an ever-increasing bloodstain. The other agent held a gun on one of the militia members. And another militia member lay motionless on the floor.

The teacher and six five-year-olds huddled in a corner. The children clung to the teacher's tunic as she used herself as a shield from all the violence. He scanned the faces of the children. They peeked out from around the teacher, eyes filled with terror. Others hid their faces altogether, snuggling into the security of the corner.

Wyatt ran over to them. "Where is Eva? Where is Christine?"

The teacher shook her head as though she couldn't process his question. "Christine?"

"Did they bring Eva's mother here?"

The teacher shook her head.

Then he heard a small voice at the teacher's feet. "They came and took Eva."

Wyatt's mind reeled. He surveyed the room again. Two militia in the hall and two in the room. That meant there were at least two more somewhere in the school. His brain clicked into high gear, and he realized that the militia member with his fingers laced behind his head and an agent's gun pointed at him was Randy.

Wyatt raced over to him and placed his face close to Randy's. "Where have they taken Christine and Eva?"

At first, Randy shook his head.

"Where have they gone?" Wyatt demanded. He searched Randy's eyes. The kid was about to crack. "Tell me. This is your chance to redeem yourself."

Randy licked his lips and let out a breath. "They went toward the library/cafeteria area."

"Where is that?"

"Up the hall and to the right." Randy's face scrunched up in agony. "I didn't mean for this to go this way."

Wyatt patted the boy's shoulder. As he left the room, he saw that the injured agent had gotten to his feet to help contain the chaos.

He grabbed the agent in the hall, who had a gun pointed at the two subdued men. "Be advised, we still have at least two men at large somewhere in this school."

"I'll help you."

"No," said Wyatt. "Get this situation contained and get these children to safety. This is not over yet. Then send in the agents to help with the extraction. I'm headed to the library."

Adrenaline surged through Wyatt's veins as he ran down the hallway and turned right. He passed bulletin boards filled with school news and children's drawings. A sign with an arrow

245

indicated where the library was. The cafeteria was across the hallway.

His senses heightened as he stepped through the open door with his gun drawn. He dived for the cover of a couch, lifting his head just high enough to take in the layout of the room. The space where he had entered the library was a lounge area with several old couches and chairs. The rest of the main floor was bookshelves that reached to the low ceiling. Across from him was the checkout counter and above him was a balcony with book-shelves and study desks. A fan whirred some-where in the room. The only other sound was his heart thudding in his ears. Even his swallow sounded as if it was on high volume. Sweat trickled down his back as he pressed his lips together.

Had Randy mislead him? Somehow, he didn't think so. The kid was being eaten alive by remorse.

He heard an odd scratching sound and then a voice filled with grit spoke. "What took you so long, Agent Green? I was sure you would come for your true love and her precious child." The voice dripped with sarcasm.

Wyatt pivoted in one direction and then in the other, trying to discern the source of the voice. It was coming through some sort of loudspeaker system. He tried to picture the blueprint of the school in his head. Where was the announcement booth?

It must be close to the library. There were doors behind the checkout counter and another back behind the main floor stacks.

" 'Course, maybe you figured you were even. She saved you at the stockyards and you saved her from the fire I had my men set."

As fast as he could move in a crouch, Wyatt scampered to the door behind the checkout counter and flung it open. It was a broom closet.

"Would you like to hear your true love?" said the voice. There was a ripping sound and then Christine's scream. She attempted to say something, but was stopped. Her words came out as an abrasive choking noise.

Wyatt cringed.

" 'Course, I wanted her to be my true love, but she wasn't interested even after her dear husband died."

"Harrison," Wyatt said under his breath. So all of this just hadn't been about some grandiose political idea. Not for him, anyway. The fight was personal for Harrison.

Out of the corner of his eye, Wyatt saw movement in the balcony. He bounded up the stairs two at a time, searching up and down the library shelves. He came out toward the balcony railing and looked out the large windows of the library that provided a view of the hallway and the cafeteria.

Wyatt's muscles tensed as rage invaded every

inch of his being. Eva sat tied up on one of the cafeteria tables with duct tape over her mouth. The announcement booth must be by the cafeteria. The man had terrorized a little girl to lure him out. He must plan on killing all three of them. Wyatt didn't care if it was a trap. He had to get to her.

As his shoe touched the top step, he sensed someone behind him. He turned. A shot fired close enough to make his eardrum pop. In the space between the books and the bottom of the eye-level shelf, he caught a view of the man's blue jeans.

He'd seen the shooter's face for a split second when he'd taken aim. It wasn't Harrison. He was tired of this game of cat and mouse. He needed to get Eva.

With one muscular heave, Wyatt pushed the bookshelf over. He heard groaning and protest as he raced down the stairs and over to the cafeteria. His boots tapped across the linoleum of the lunchroom. Relief replaced the fear in Eva's eyes as he approached. He untied her hands first. Her arms went around him and she held tight. Even with the duct tape over her mouth, whimpering sounds escaped.

Wyatt glanced from side to side, aiming his pistol with his free hand as he held her and backed away. The man in the library had managed to dig himself out from under the books and was headed down the stairs. Wyatt ducked with Eva behind a serving cart.

Where were the other agents? They should have gotten the hostages out by now and taken the perpetrators into custody. Unless something had gone wrong.

Wyatt spoke very gently to Eva. "I'm going to take the tape off your mouth so you can tell me where your mom is. It will hurt, but I want you to be brave."

Though tears streamed down her face, Eva nodded.

"You're strong, just like your mom."

He'd just gotten the tape off when a door slammed. Eva blinked and took in a sharp breath. Wyatt placed his finger over his lips in a shushing motion.

"Where is the girl?" It was Harrison's voice. He was in the cafeteria.

The man in the library came down the stairs and made his way toward the cafeteria holding a gun.

Harrison stomped across the lunchroom. His voice filled with rage, he let out a string of curses.

The man from the library was seconds away from entering the cafeteria. He'd spot Eva and Wyatt behind the cart when he stepped across the threshold. Wyatt couldn't see Harrison, but he made a guess at where he was based on his voice.

Wyatt pointed at a planter and whispered to Eva, "Go now, hide."

As the man came through the door, Wyatt rose to his feet and aimed his gun while kicking the food cart in the direction he thought Harrison was. The single shot took the man down. Wyatt turned to see a stunned Harrison raising his gun. Christine ducked behind the cart.

Wyatt took aim. Harrison turned to run. Christine grabbed his leg at the ankle, and he toppled to the floor.

Two more agents converged on the cafeteria from opposite sides of the hallway. Wyatt scrambled over to Harrison to restrain him. He addressed the two agents who wrestled with the other militia member.

More agents ran by in the hallway.

"Took you long enough," said Wyatt.

"We met with a little resistance on our way out. A gunman we didn't account for, who had been hiding."

"Is everyone okay?" Wyatt held his breath, afraid of what the answer might be.

"Children and teacher got out alive."

Relief spread through him as Christine scrambled across the floor to him. He reached out to touch the fresh scratch on her face. "You okay?"

Christine shook off the question. Her voice filled with desperation. "Where is she?"

Wyatt pointed toward the planter. "You can come out now, Eva."

Mother and daughter ran toward each other, both gulping and tearful as they hugged. Wyatt kept his gun on Harrison as longing to embrace the two females who mattered most to him hit him with full force. As he watched Christine stroke Eva's hair and whisper to her, he felt a tug at his heart. They were his family.

The second agent ran over to where Wyatt held the gun on Harrison while he lay facedown on the floor. "I can get him cuffed and taken out. Why don't you go join them?"

As he walked toward them, Eva held her arms out to him, her face glowing. His heart warmed. He took her in his arms and Christine leaned against his shoulder.

Eva's soft hand brushed over Wyatt's neck like a butterfly's wing. "Mr. Wyatt saved us."

"Your mom helped quite a bit. She can handle herself just fine."

Christine tilted her head. A faint smiled crossed her lips. Her eyes filled with affection. "It was a team effort."

"I wouldn't have known where to look for you if it hadn't been for Randy," Wyatt said.

"I'm glad he came through. He should get a reduced sentence for that. It will be a comfort to his mom to know that he tried to make things right. I will tell her myself."

As they were leaving with the last two militia members, one of the agents turned back toward them. "They are taking everyone involved to the hospital to get statements."

"I suppose we should get over there," said Christine.

As they walked out together, Wyatt prayed for the right moment to tell Christine he loved her.

NINETEEN

The normally quiet hospital resembled Grand Central Station. People were being called back to exam rooms. An injured militia member was restrained on a gurney and wheeled out of sight. Newspeople pushed through the crowd with microphones and cameras. Parents searched for and embraced their children in the waiting room. Laughter and crying swirled through the commotion. Deputy Mitchell stood beside Agent Cranson as they took the teacher's statement together. Other agents milled through the crowd.

A man wearing a baseball hat that said FBI came up to Wyatt. "Green, we're going to need your help on this." He pulled Wyatt away before he could object. The backward glance he gave Christine was filled with helplessness.

The warmth of Wyatt's hand holding hers slipped away as he was absorbed into the crowd. Even though Eva pressed close to her, a sense of loss prevailed when she could no longer see him.

Maggie pushed her way through the crowd.

Eva gave a yell of glee and ran to her grand-mother. Maggie held out her free arm for Christine and embraced her. Clusters of people jostled around them.

Maggie whispered in her ear, "My precious daughter-in-law. You have no idea how glad I am to see you two."

Christine's throat constricted. She had no words to explain the gratitude that flowed through her. She hugged Maggie tighter.

"It's hot in here," said Eva as people pressed in on her.

Both women laughed.

"We should go outside to get some air," suggested Maggie.

Christine pressed the older woman's arm. "I'll join you in just a minute. I need to find Wyatt."

Maggie gathered Eva into her arms and made her way toward the door.

Christine pushed through the crowd in the direction she had seen Wyatt go. The crowd thinned as she moved away from the waiting room into a corridor. No sign of Wyatt. Her need to be with him overwhelmed her.

Lonnie came out of a hospital room and offered her a big grin. He grabbed her hand and shook it vigorously. "I just heard. You did good, Sheriff Norris."

"Thank you." Christine caught a glimpse of a

white-haired woman in a hospital bed. "Is your wife doing okay?"

"She is now." Lonnie couldn't stop grinning.

Christine shook her head. "I'm sorry. I don't know what you mean."

"It was Irene's nephew who was shot ten years ago. Her sister's boy."

"Oh." Different last names and the sister must have left town shortly after she moved here. She'd never made the connection.

"After the bomb blast, when it looked like the town would be swarming with agents, she spiraled back into a depression," Lonnie explained.

A realization hit her. "That was you in my hospital room that night."

A look of shame clouded his features. "Please, I was panicked. I was only trying to protect my wife. But it's all right now."

Christine nodded. "Maybe we can all finally get beyond this as a town."

Lonnie winked, patted her shoulder and turned to go into the hospital room.

"Just give me a minute." Wyatt's voice floated from around the corner.

Christine ran toward the sound of his voice. She met his gaze as he closed the hospital director's office that was probably being used as a make-shift command station for processing all the information and evidence coming in.

They were the only two people in the corridor.

"I was going to go looking for you," he said.

"You found me." The look of love in his eyes was like a magnet pulling her toward him.

"I wanted you to know—" he gathered her in his arms and he searched her eyes "—that I love you."

She wrapped her arms around his neck. "Oh, Wyatt. I know. Your actions have shown me who you are. You didn't have to say it."

"Yes, I did have to say it." His hand stroked her hair. "It doesn't matter where we live or what I do as long as I am with you and Eva. I want to be your husband and Eva's father if you will have me."

She managed to whisper "yes." He cupped his fingers under her chin and tilted her head. His lips covered hers and lingered for a long time until she was breathless. Wyatt smiled and drew her closer. His strong arms comforted her as joy bubbled up and she knew she was right where she needed to be.

Dear Reader,

Broken Trust was a great title for this book in more ways than one. Not only does Wyatt need to repair the trust he destroyed ten years ago with Christine, but the town where Christine lives also needs healing. The citizens of Roosevelt, Montana, feel they can no longer trust the FBI because of a tragic incident in the past. While the book is about Wyatt and Christine healing from the pain of the past, it's also about how the townspeople forge a new identity.

I hope you enjoyed Christine and Wyatt's love story. Both of them had to take risks and open their hearts in order for them to be together. As I was writing the book, I thought about how all relationships, if they are to deepen, involve risk. Not only in a romantic sense, but even with friendships and relationships with children. If we are to grow closer, we have to risk being hurt.

God designed us to be connected to other people, and yet sometimes our past experience and our fear of being hurt get in the way of that. I think the final reason why having the word *trust* in the title was such a great choice was that ultimately we have to trust God, that when relationships don't work out or we are wounded, He is the safety net. Even when people let us down, He does not.

Best wishes,

Sharon Dunn

Questions for Discussion

1. What was the most exciting scene for you in the story?

2. Why are the people in town reluctant to trust or help the FBI?

3. Which character did you identify with? Why?

4. Wyatt chooses to use actions rather than words to reveal to Christine that he has changed. What does Wyatt do that helps Christine see that he is emotionally ready to be a father and a husband?

5. Have you ever had to win someone's trust back after a relationship became broken? What specific things did you do? Is there anything you wish you would have done differently?

6. Even though she is a widow, Christine has support in her job, her home and the community. Who helps Christine and how has it made her feel as if she belongs?

7. What kind of childhood did Wyatt have? How did it affect his relationships as an adult?

8. As Wyatt works with Christine he starts to see the value of family and community, something he has never had. Can you name some specific moments when this revelation comes to Wyatt?

9. Does the town of Roosevelt remind you of anyplace you have visited or lived in? Were there any characters who reminded you of someone you knew?

10. Though both Christine and Wyatt are in law-enforcement professions, their roles are not alike. In what way were their jobs different? In what ways were they similar?

11. Why was the character of Randy Stiller vulnerable to being recruited into a radical group? Could he have made different choices?

12. Sometimes when we have been deeply hurt it's hard to take risks again and to trust people or situations. Can you recall a time when you had to risk being hurt or anxious or afraid in order to grow or heal?

13. Although the fire was a tragic loss, it led Christine to some discoveries about herself. What are those revelations? Have you ever made discoveries or grown because of a loss similar to Christine's?

14. At what points in the story do you see Christine let go of Dustin and the past? Do you think this needed to happen in order for her to fully commit to Wyatt?

15. Christine and Wyatt's love story spans over ten years. Have you ever been reunited with someone, in love or friendship, after not seeing them for many years? Did old feelings, both positive and negative, rise to the surface? Were there things that needed to be talked about and resolved, or was it as if you had never been apart?

About the Author

SHARON DUNN has always loved writing, but didn't decide to write for publication until she was expecting her first baby. Pregnancy makes you do crazy things. Three kids, many articles and two mystery series later, she still hasn't found her sanity. Her books have won awards, including a Book of the Year Award from American Christian Fiction Writers. She was also a finalist for an *RT Book Reviews* Inspirational Book of the Year Award.

Sharon has performed in theater and church productions, has degrees in film production and history and worked for many years as a college tutor and instructor. Despite the fact that her résumé looks as if she couldn't decide what she wanted to be when she grew up, all the education and experience have played a part in helping her write good stories.

When she isn't writing or taking her kids to activities, she reads, plays board games and contemplates organizing her closet. In addition to her three kids, Sharon lives with her husband of twenty-two years, three cats and lots of dust bunnies. You can reach Sharon through her website at www.sharondunnbooks.net.

Center Point Large Print
600 Brooks Road / PO Box 1
Thorndike ME 04986-0001 USA

(207) 568-3717

US & Canada:
1 800 929-9108
www.centerpointlargeprint.com